CAPITOL
KILLER

(Tracy Sterling Book 2)

By RJ Law

Chapter 1

Tony watched from across the street as the maid shuffled from one motel room to the next. Between them, cars zoomed by on a busy two-lane road, their blurry shapes briefly interrupting his view as he peeked around a thick oak tree.

While the vehicle engines roared and then faded, the Mexican woman wheeled along a little cart stocked with white towels and big bottles of bleach. All the while, Tony's eyes traveled the length of her short, waddling body, the hairnet on her scalp suppressing what appeared to be a formidable avalanche of inky-black hair.

He ran his tongue over a pair of thin lips and narrowed his eyes. She looked to be in her late forties, and her figure had gone to fat. But he wasn't the picky type. And there was something about her pale blue uniform that congested his mind with lewd thoughts.

He waited and watched as she tapped a small fist against one of the motel room doors, his small eager body squirming like someone waiting outside a locked bathroom door.

"Housekeeping," she must have said. But Tony couldn't hear her over the traffic.

She knocked again, but no one answered the door. She knocked a third time and waited a few seconds longer before withdrawing a little keycard. Tony watched as she opened the door and forced her cart inside.

When the door closed behind her, he threw a glance over his shoulder and then carefully navigated the stream of traffic, one car honking madly as it slowed to miss him.

When Tony reached the other side, he withdrew a slip of paper from his pocket and double-checked the room number. Then, he moved along the little strip of motel rooms, his small eyes squinting up at the numbers in search of a match.

When he found the right room, he straightened his collar and ran a hand over his greasy, slicked-back hair. Then, he cleared his throat and pounded his fist against the door.

"Hotel staff!" he shrieked. "This is an emergency!"

He paused and strained to listen. Inside, panicked shuffling mixed with indecipherable mumbling. Someone ordered someone else to be quiet. Heavy footsteps approached the door.

"Open up, now!" Tony cried as he beat the door again. "We're running out of time! This is a matter of life and death!"

He heard the metallic sound of locks disengaging and straightened his body just as the door cracked open an inch. A large probing eye appeared in the thin crease and assessed the short, weasely-looking man.

"What is it?" said a gravelly male voice.

Tony's face pinched in with concern, and the eye seemed to flinch at his pointy, rat-like appearance.

"We've got an emergency here. You need to exit the room."

With a sudden motion, Tony put his hand on the door and pushed inward.

"Hey!" yelled the man.

He stumbled backward as the door flung open, his hand clutching a white cotton sheet against his naked body. Behind him, a very attractive woman did the same, her sheet struggling to conceal the volume of her great jiggling breasts.

Tony leered at her for a moment and then regained his composure.

"I'm sorry, sir," he said. "I'm gonna have to ask you and the lady to exit the room."

"What?"

Tony pointed a finger at him.

"We've got a serious gas leak, and we need to get the two of you clear before the fire department arrives."

The man raised his chin and snorted the air.

"I don't smell anything."

Tony shrugged.

"Well, it's the carbon monoxide you have to worry about. You can't smell that stuff."

The woman furrowed her brow.

"But wouldn't we smell gas if there was a leak?"

Tony gave a couple of quick sniffs.

"You can't smell that?"

The man lowered his eyebrows.

"No."

Tony willed the color from his face.

"Goodness, if that's the case, you've likely acclimated to it. This means you may have inhaled a dangerous amount. We need to get both of you out in the fresh air immediately."

The man took a step back.

"Well, hold on a minute and let us get dressed."

Tony shook his head and reached for the man's arm.

"I'm sorry, there's no time. There's a high risk of an explosion. You need to evacuate right this second."

"Now, hold on," said the man. "Let me just find my pants."

Tony turned away and held a hand over his ear.

"Yes, sir," he said as he looked at the ground. "Yes, sir, I understand an explosion is imminent. But one of the guests is giving me trouble. Do you want me to use the Taser?"

The man looked back at the woman who had lost some color in her face.

"Now, wait a second," said the man. "That won't be necessary."

He turned toward the woman who was now frantically sniffing the room.

"Come on, Brittney."

Tony stepped aside and let them pass, his eyes stealing a glance at the woman's buttocks as she scampered out into the parking lot.

Cars slowed as the two stood next to the street dressed awkwardly in their white sheets, as if they were roadside actors performing a Shakespearean play. Tony trailed behind them, his eyes glancing between the half-nude woman and a small parking lot on the other side of the road.

"Aren't you going to evacuate the other rooms?" the man asked, while he and the woman frantically breathed the fresh air.

4

Tony raised a finger.

"Gimme a second."

A car slowed, and the driver hooted out his open window. The woman clutched her sheet while the man's face colored.

"This is ridiculous!" he said. "What is going on?"

Tony looked at him and shrugged.

"You know what? My mistake."

The man's face took on a deeper shade of red as he stared at the little man.

"What?"

Tony shrugged and gave a friendly smile.

"You two have a nice day."

With that, he walked away, his hands in his pockets as he whistled a little tune.

"What?" the man shouted again.

"Come on, Michael," said the woman. "I'm cold."

They watched the strange little man make his way across the street and disappear behind a big tree. Then, they shook their heads and went back into the motel room.

Tony waited until they shut themselves inside. Then, he trotted across the little parking lot to a small sedan, where Tracy Sterling sat with her camera, a bored look on her tired face.

"You got what you need?" Tony asked as he sidled up to her window.

Tracy turned off the camera and slipped it into her bag.

"Yep."

Tony stuck his hands in his coat pockets and looked back across the street.

"So, what's it all about? You blackmailing this guy or somethin?"

Tracy glared at him.

"He's having an affair. His wife paid me to follow him."

He licked his lips and watched as she withdrew two one-hundred-dollar bills.

"Thanks for the help," she said as she passed the cash through the open window.

He took the money and held it up to the sun, like a jeweler inspecting gemstones for the subtlest flaws. When he was satisfied, he shoved the money into a pocket and regarded her with a smile that made his face hard to look at.

"I don't want to offend you, but this seems like some kind of small-time hustle. You ever want to make some real money; I got some lucrative ideas."

Tracy sighed.

"I'm sure you do."

He shrugged.

"I mean, just speaking hypothetically, if you were to meet me at the docks tomorrow—"

"No thanks," she said. "Anyway, I have to be in court all day."

He raised his eyebrows.

"Oh, yeah. I know how it is." He shrugged his bony shoulders and smiled. "Well, keep my number anyway. I never turn down a few easy bucks."

She nodded and started her car while he watched her with raised eyebrows.

"If you don't mind me askin, how much does somethin like this pay anyway? I mean, this kind of surveillance bullshit or whatever you want to call it?"

She shook her head.

"About a month of rent. Maybe."

He frowned down at her.

"You ever think about another line of work?"

She turned toward the road.

"All the time."

Bradley looked around the room like a caged wolf, his eyes wide as he assessed his uncertain surroundings. Imposing and grandiose, the great courtroom was a study in contrasts. Floored with green marble tile, it had an air of stern refinement that seemed ill-balanced by the dark mahogany furniture, which did little to temper the room's cold austerity.

The clash of styles extended to the gallery, where a hodgepodge of diverse faces watched with rapt attention, their ordinary clothes seeming ill-suited for such a stately setting.

But it was Bradley who truly seemed out of place. Heavier than ever, he wore a cheap suit that stretched thin against the girth of his body. And as he breathed through an open mouth, his attorney passed over a handkerchief for the sweat dripping off his chin.

While his client mopped the secretions from his flabby neck, the attorney shuffled through a stack of papers, his distinguished face completely relaxed as Tracy approached the stand.

Middle-aged and gray-haired, the lawyer seemed to be a man of friendly intentions. But to Tracy's keen eyes, he was a serpent in a suit. A seasoned liar honed by years of legal jousting, who would use words of honey and poison to undermine her credibility at every turn.

With folded hands, the attorney waited patiently for Tracy to give her oath and sit. Then, he stood up and smiled.

"Thank you for being here today," he said as he approached. "Can you please state your name?"

"Tracy Sterling."

"And you are the daughter of the late Robert Sterling. Is that correct?"

"Yes."

"That would be former Detective Robert Sterling?"

"Yes."

The attorney held up a sheet of paper and squinted at the text. Then, his eyes widened as if he'd just made a shocking discovery.

"The same Detective Robert Sterling who was recently linked to several criminal offenses, including multiple instances of obstruction of justice, evidence tampering and conspiracy. Is that also correct?"

At the other table, the district attorney stood.

"Objection. Your Honor, Ms. Sterling is not responsible for the actions of her relatives, and her record as a detective was spotless."

Bearded and quite old, the judge loomed over the proceedings with an expressionless face. But when he spoke, his voice rang through the courtroom like the bong of a huge brass bell.

"Overruled. But be careful, Mr. Hobbes."

The attorney gave a polite smile.

"Of course, Your Honor."

He looked at Tracy, who watched him with a cold, emotionless expression.

"Now, Ms. Sterling. Do you deny my previous statement?"

Tracy raised her eyebrows.

"No. But I was the one who—"

" 'No' is all I need, Ms. Sterling. Thank you."

7

The attorney turned his back on Tracy and approached the jury box, a pleasant smile on his face, as if he were exactly where he wished to be at this exact moment on this particular day.

"Now," he said without looking back, "during your very brief stint as a police detective, who were you partnered with?"

Tracy leaned toward the microphone.

"Gary Johnson."

"Mm hm," said the attorney as he looked upon the jurors. "And would this be the same Gary Johnson who was also recently linked to multiple instances of obstruction of justice, evidence planting and conspiracy?"

The DA stood.

"Objection, Your Honor. This is irrelevant. Ms. Sterling is not the one on trial here."

The attorney turned away from the jury and held his palms upward, his face assuming a look of unquestionable innocence.

"I'm merely asking questions about the witness's background, Your Honor. If she was trained by corrupt police officers or exposed to their techniques, this may speak to her credibility as a witness today."

"Overruled," said the judge. "The witness will answer the question."

The attorney regarded Tracy with a smug little smirk.

"Ms. Sterling?"

Tracy flexed her jaw and leaned toward the microphone.

"Yes. Gary Johnson was my partner during my time as a police detective."

The attorney turned back toward the jury and held his arms out to his side.

"And now Gary Johnson is not a detective anymore. And neither are you. Interesting."

"Objection."

The judge frowned.

"Sustained. Please interview the witness and refrain from addressing the jury, Mr. Hobbes."

"My apologies, Your Honor."

The attorney approached Tracy and settled directly before her, his eyes bright and blue and twinkling with malice.

"Alright, Ms. Sterling," he said in a low velvety voice. "Now that we've established exactly who you are, let's move on to how you know my client."

He pursed his lips as if he were struggling to find the right words for a sensitive topic.

"Now, you worked with Bradley Myers for a little less than two years. Is that correct?"

"Yes."

The attorney raised an eyebrow.

"And how would you characterize your relationship? Were you good friends?"

Tracy gave no reaction, her face entirely closed.

"No."

The attorney pushed his lower lip out.

"You didn't hang out after work? Go see movies together? Perhaps an occasional lunch to discuss the specifics of a case?"

Tracy stared into his bright, beaming eyes.

"No."

The attorney turned away from her and clasped his hands behind his back.

"Isn't it true, Ms. Sterling, that you hold significant animosity toward my client? In fact, haven't you expressed your hatred for him on multiple occasions?"

"Objection."

The attorney approached his table and collected a stack of papers. He turned and held them up in the air as he approached the judge.

"Your Honor, I have statements from several of Ms. Sterling's former co-workers detailing numerous occasions where she openly expressed her contempt for my client."

The judge eyed the papers and frowned.

"Overruled."

The attorney grinned as he turned toward Tracy.

"Now, Ms. Sterling, do I need to read these to the court?"

Tracy looked up at the attorney and shrugged.

"That won't be necessary," she said as she leaned toward the microphone. "No, Mr. Myers and I are not close friends. I do, in fact, hold him in contempt as I would any police officer who would tamper with evidence."

The attorney gave a tight-lipped frown, as if Tracy had unexpectedly parried his death blow. But he quickly recovered and prepared another strike.

"Ok, Ms. Sterling. Since you brought it up, let's entertain this little theory of yours."

Tracy glowered at him.

"It's not my theory. It's the view of the state."

The attorney gave a condescending smile.

"Fine. Let's dig into this view of the state."

He said the last few words with a sarcastic tone as he rolled his eyes at the jury.

"Now," he continued, "my client is accused of planting evidence to lead investigators into misidentifying a potential murder suspect. And, according to you, he accomplished this by somehow acquiring a hair from Grace Crawford's corpse and placing it at the home of an Anthony Garcia, who was initially charged with the murder of Ms. Crawford. Have I got all that right?"

"Yes."

He put his hands out to his side and furrowed his eyebrows.

"Now, why would he do something like that?"

Tracy shrugged.

"I wouldn't know."

"No?" asked the attorney as he drew closer. "Come on, Ms. Sterling, surely you can think of something? Not even a guess?"

Tracy raised her eyebrows and met his eye.

"Maybe it was his usual way of doing things. I'm not a corrupt cop, so I wouldn't know."

The attorney showed his teeth a little as if he'd taken another wound. Then, he forced another smile and turned away.

"Alright, then. We've established that you don't know. That's enough for me."

He approached Bradley and took up another sheet of paper. He held it up and skimmed it over. Then, he turned back toward Tracy, who watched him with her boredest expression.

"Now," said the attorney. "Let's move to the actual murder itself."

He put a finger to his chin and looked at her thoughtfully, as if they were a team working out a mutual problem together.

"Now, according to police records, this Anthony Garcia was ultimately released, and all charges were dropped. Is that correct?"

10

"Yes."

"And why was that? I mean, considering they found some of Grace Crawford's hair at his house, it does seem odd."

Tracy leaned closer to the microphone.

"It was ultimately determined that the more compelling evidence pointed to someone else."

The attorney tapped his finger against his chin and frowned. "Interesting."

He turned and pointed a finger at Bradley, who could not keep the hate from his eyes.

"So, if my client did not plant this hair, that would make you and your little team wrong. How embarrassing."

Tracy said nothing, and her face seemed to say less.

"Now," said the attorney, "in the course of your investigation, you surmised that Grace Crawford was murdered by Tim Cooper, also identified as the infamous Alleyway Killer. Is this correct?"

Tracy nodded.

"That was the consensus of the team investigating the case. And I agreed based on the available evidence."

The attorney gave a nod as if he, too, agreed with this assessment.

"And did you ultimately acquire any evidence confirming your theory? DNA? Something like that?"

Tracy paused for a moment, and the attorney's eyes seemed to twinkle.

"Ms. Sterling?"

Tracy leaned closer to the microphone.

"It is my understanding that investigators found a good deal of evidence implicating Tim Cooper's involvement in the Alleyway murders during an extensive search of his home."

Like a cat perched outside a mouse hole, the attorney prepared to pounce.

"Oh," he said. "So, they must have found something linking Tim Cooper to Grace Crawford then. Some DNA evidence? A hair, perhaps?"

Tracy flexed her jaw.

"Not to my knowledge."

As if truly offended, the attorney put both hands on his hips and lowered his eyebrows.

"Now, hold on a second. You're telling me, you decided that Tim Cooper was responsible for Grace Crawford's murder without any evidence implicating him in the crime?"

Tracy narrowed her eyes.

"No. That is not what I'm saying."

The attorney put one arm out to his side and raised his eyebrows.

"Well, then, you must have some good reason for your little theory. A confession, perhaps?"

Tracy firmed her mouth.

"No."

The attorney looked dumbstruck.

"No confession? Well, I suppose that's understandable. After all, he would have been facing multiple counts of murder. That must have made him a tough nut to crack. Is that an accurate assessment of your difficulties withdrawing a confession?"

Tracy chewed her teeth.

"No."

As if he had finally lost all patience, the attorney dropped both arms to his side.

"Well, then, why do you suppose you weren't able to get a confession, Ms. Sterling? I mean, supposing Tim Cooper was responsible, and considering his apparent desire to attract attention for his actions, why wouldn't he just come right out and admit to it?"

Tracy's eyes made an involuntary movement toward the jury before she could catch herself.

"We were not able to interview Mr. Cooper."

"Oh," said the attorney. "That's too bad. And why was that?"

Tracy steadied herself with a slow breath and then leaned closer to the microphone.

"Mr. Cooper did not survive the rescue of Elizabeth Gannon."

The attorney raised his eyebrows and pointed toward Tracy.

"Because you killed him. Isn't that correct?"

The DA leaped to her feet.

"Objection. Your Honor, Ms. Sterling fired her weapon as a last resort in an act of self-defense and as part of a heroic effort to save the life of a kidnap victim. Now, I want the record to show that she has been fully cleared of any wrongdoing and has received a commendation for bravery for her actions. This line of questioning is out of bounds and completely irrelevant to this case."

The judge glared at the attorney.

"Sustained," he said with his gong of a voice. "Mr. Hobbes, I've given you considerable leeway, but there is an end to my patience."

Like a humble servant at the feet of a great king, the attorney bowed and took a step back.

"My apologies, Your Honor."

He frowned at the floor for several seconds and then raised his head toward Tracy.

"One last question, Ms. Sterling." He approached and frowned down at her with a look of genuine pity. "What do you do these days? I mean, now that you're not a detective, how do you pay the bills?"

Tracy straightened in her seat and squared her shoulders.

"I work as a private investigator."

"Oh," said the attorney. "How interesting. So, what does that mean exactly? You follow around cheating husbands and snap photos of injured people trying to prove insurance fraud?"

He smiled and waited for a response, his eyes dancing as he looked down on her with brazen self-satisfaction. Tacy looked back at him through bold, unflinching eyes.

"It varies. Sometimes I'm hired by people who have been falsely accused by corrupt cops."

The attorney glared at her.

"Oh, I'm sure," he said as he turned away. "No further questions."

As he made his way back to his table, the DA stood and addressed Tracy.

"Ms. Sterling, you received a commendation for single-handedly apprehending the serial murderer known as the Alleyway Killer. Is that correct?"

"Yes."

"And in the process, you rescued Elizabeth Gannon, who had been held captive for weeks by Tim Cooper. Is that correct?"

"Yes."

"And the hallmark of Mr. Cooper was to pin one of the victim's hands to the torso using a nail. Is this also correct?"

"Yes."

"And was Grace Crawford's hand pinned to her torso in the same fashion?

"That is correct."

The DA glanced at the defense attorney who was whispering to Bradley.

"And, Ms. Sterling," she continued, "In your expert opinion, could this be a copycat situation? In other words, could this Anthony Garcia have possibly seen something on the news that inspired him to mimic Tim Cooper?"

"No," said Tracy. "The media was aware of some details of the case. But they did not know that any of the victims' hands had been pinned to their torsos. The only people who knew that detail were the detectives working the case and the killer himself. The evidence is clear that Tim Cooper killed Grace Crawford, and any physical evidence found at Anthony Garcia's home must have been planted by the defendant."

"Thank you, Ms. Sterling. No further questions."

The judge dismissed Tracy and ordered a recess, while murmurs spread through the gallery like a contagion.

As she stepped down and crossed the floor, Tracy felt the heat of Bradley's stare. Without acknowledging him, she made her way down the aisle that split the gallery. But a voice stopped her as she put a hand against the door.

"Ms. Sterling?"

Tracy turned to see a short, middle-aged man in a tailored suit. "Yes?"

"My name is Andrew Stallings. Can we speak outside?"

A headache had bloomed up in Tracy's head, and she regarded the man with a frown.

"What about?"

He raised his eyebrows.

"A business opportunity."

She looked past him and saw Bradley staring at her from across the room, his eyes trained on her face as if he meant to set it afire.

"I suppose," she told the man.

They stepped through the doors and stood together out in the hall.

"Who are you exactly?" she asked as she rubbed her temples.

"The name's Andrew Stallings. I'm an attorney for Senator Paul Jenkins.

Tracy looked the man over. He was mostly bald except for a few gray tufts of hair horseshoeing their way around his head. He wore eyeglasses that gave him a scholarly look, and he held a newspaper

14

under one arm. He did not smile, nor did he frown, but he seemed friendly enough in a passionless, professional sort of way.

"What can I do for you, Mr. Stallings?"

"I might have some work for you, if you're interested."

Tracy shrugged.

"Sure. I have a card somewhere here."

She patted her jacket, and he shook his head.

"That won't be necessary. I already have all your information."

She looked up at him and furrowed her brow.

"Alright," she said. "What kind of job are we talking about?"

Mr. Stallings firmed his lips.

"I'm not really at liberty to provide the details at this time. Considering my client's high profile, I'm sure it won't surprise you to learn that it's an especially sensitive issue. We'd like to meet with you before making a decision."

Tracy raised her eyebrows.

"Well, I am quite busy right now," she lied.

"We understand," said Mr. Stallings. "Your time is valuable, and Senator Jenkins is willing to pay a very competitive rate to acquire your services."

"Ok," said Tracy. "What can you tell me?"

"Only that this is a timely issue, so we'd like to get started right away. Can you meet with our team this evening?"

Tracy considered her calendar and decided the television could wait.

"I suppose," she said, doing her best to feign an appropriate amount of irritation.

Mr. Stallings withdrew a card from his pocket and handed it to her.

"Please arrive at this address at 8 p.m. this evening. Dress professionally." He eyed her from head to toe. "This here will do fine."

Tracy followed his eyes to her clothing and then looked up at him.

"Oh, good," she said flatly.

Oblivious to her sarcasm, Mr. Stallings gave a nod and offered a weak smile.

"By the way, I think you performed quite well up there. That was a bear trap, and you gave as good as you got."

Tracy gave him a polite nod.

"Thank you."

He returned her nod and walked away, his eyes glancing at his watch as he exited the building. Tracy watched through the glass doors as the lawyer met up with a tall, thin man in a black suit. The two stood together chatting for a moment, Stallings shrugging several times as the tall man appeared to pepper him with questions. Then, the two walked away together, the lawyer frowning down at the pavement while the other man continued to speak, his face disturbingly gaunt and tight with obvious frustration.

Tracy watched until both men disappeared around the corner of a building. Then, she left the courthouse and made the long drive home.

Chapter 2

It was a quarter to eight by the time Tracy reached the senator's estate, and the last of the daylight had dwindled to nothing at the edge of a blushing horizon. With a slow, deliberate pace, she wheeled her car off the main road and made her way down the long drive, where an ornate wrought-iron gate waited to block her way. Next to the tall gate, edging the path, an armed security man stood outside a little brick shed, his eyes squinting into her headlights as she approached.

Meticulously pruned and groomed, the senator's property was carved from a little forest of trees, which surrounded the manicured grounds like wardens as they soared into the blackening heavens. As Tracy approached the security man, she felt those trees close in around her, and something vague in her chest urged her to turn back.

"ID?" asked the security man as she pulled up.

Tracy passed over her driver's license through the open window.

"I'm expected," she said.

The security man held the license up to her face.

"Yes," he said. "Go ahead."

The gate inched open, and she drove up the winding path, which cut through a courtyard toward a small but stately mansion. All around her, little trees dotted the landscape, an evening wind tickling their leaves, which twinkled in the moonlight like falling coins.

As her car rolled up the lengthy drive, she passed below the arching branches of cherry blossom trees, which hung in the night sky like a string of pink clouds. Almost involuntarily, Tracy slowed to appreciate their little petals, which perfumed the air as the wind nipped them free and scattered them like confetti atop the evenly cut green grass.

At last, she pulled to a stop and cracked open her door. With a sudden rush, the sweet scent of spring flowers filled her nostrils, evoking memories of childhood picnics and lazy afternoons in the sun. She shook these thoughts away and stepped out of the car.

Without hesitating, she climbed the steps and approached the front of the stately structure which loomed before her like the entrance to some great hall. A large brass knocker hung from the middle of the imposing oak door, and she reached to grasp it before noticing the doorbell. With a quick jab, she poked the glowing button and stepped back while a series of bells and chimes exploded within the interior of the mansion.

Footsteps clapped the floor as someone approached the door from the other side. Tracy straightened her posture in preparation for a stuffy English butler. But instead, when the door swung open, she saw the senator's lawyer, who greeted her with the same passionless face he wore at the courthouse.

"Ms. Sterling," he said.

"Mr. Stallings," she replied.

He looked her up and down and nodded.

"This way, please."

He stepped aside and shut the door behind them. Tracy paused and looked around. The foyer was grand, with a sweeping staircase leading up to the second floor. Above her head, a great chandelier hung from the ceiling, its glittering crystal drops casting reflections throughout the room. The walls were adorned with intricate tapestries and ornate mirrors, and below her feet, marble floors that glimmered in the dim light.

Tracy gave a low whistle.

"Politics is a lucrative business, I guess."

The lawyer frowned at her.

"I suppose."

She looked at him.

"Is part of your job tending to the senator's front door?"

Mr. Stallings shook his head.

"The senator is out of town, and the grounds are mostly unstaffed right now."

Tracy raised her eyebrows.

"I was under the impression I would be meeting with the senator."

"No," said Stallings. "We'll be handling this matter on his behalf. If all goes well, you won't be meeting Senator Jenkins at all."

"I see," said Tracy. "Well, what is this all about then?"

The lawyer shook his head.

"We'll get to that if necessary. But first, come with me."

He set off toward a door on the far side of the room, his shoes clacking the hard marble floor as he hurried away. Tracy gave one last look at her surroundings and shook her head a little as she hurried to catch up. When he reached the other side of the foyer, Stallings opened a door into a long curving hallway.

"This way," he said.

Tracy followed him down the hallway, her shoes crushing a thick burgundy carpet that would have seemed ostentatious in any other setting. As they moved, they passed more tapestries, where serious-looking men frowned out from their places along the walls. In a nook that seemed specifically made for its purpose, a marble bust of what appeared to be a Roman emperor sat atop a pedestal, the carved face looking stoic as its sightless eyes watched her pass.

Tracy started to speak but stopped when Stallings halted before another door.

"Please step in here and wait with the others. It should only be a few minutes."

"Others?" asked Tracy.

"I'll explain later," he said. "Now, please."

He gestured to the door again, and Tracy shrugged.

"It's your dollar."

She reached for the knob and opened the door. Inside, she saw an elegant meeting room with a long polished conference table. Seated at the table were three rough-looking men, who seemed more suited for a seedy bar than a mansion.

Tracy looked them over, and they looked back, their faces pinched tight with what seemed like angry intensity.

"What is this?" she asked.

"I'll explain everything in a moment," said Stallings. "Just have a seat for now."

He turned to leave and then stopped.

"And please don't communicate with these men."

Tracy started to respond, but he had already shut the door. She sighed and turned toward the men who scrutinized her through narrow eyes. Feigning a cool, unconcerned demeanor, she forced herself to take a seat on a distant side of the table, several seats away from the men.

While they watched, she sat back in her chair and drummed her fingers against the table, an expensive item that appeared to be made of hard maple. By sheer will, she forced a yawn that made her seem relaxed and completely unperturbed, as if she sat with close friends on the most ordinary of days.

One of the men shook his head.

"Now, they got a broad in here, too?" he said in a thick Jersey accent.

One of the other men looked at him.

"Hey, they said not to talk."

The first man shrugged.

"I don't give a fuck. This is some bush-league shit. And I'm gettin sick of it."

The third member of the group scratched his whiskered jaw and assessed Tracy, who shuddered on the inside as his eyes traveled over her skin.

"Wait a second," he said with a gravelly voice. "Ain't you that lady from TV?"

The other two men looked at Tracy thoughtfully.

"Yeah," said Jersey voice. "I saw you on TV. You're that cop that shot that college boy. The one that killed all those hookers."

The other men looked at Tracy with horror.

"They got a cop in here?" said the second man. "What the hell is this shit?"

Tracy started to speak, but the door swung open.

"Ms. Sterling," said Stallings. "We're ready for you."

With a casual air, Tracy stood up and dusted her hands together. Then, she looked at the men and smiled.

"Gentlemen," she said.

The three men watched her with unamused glares as she followed Stallings out of the room and shut the door behind her.

"What the hell is going on?" asked Tracy as she followed the lawyer down the hallway.

"I must apologize," said Stallings. "I can't really explain right now. Please be patient. I'll answer all your questions in due time."

They continued down the hallway until they came to another door that looked very much like the one from before. Sure enough, when Stallings opened the door, he revealed a nearly identical room, appointed with another long conference table surrounded by empty seats.

Tracy peered into the room and saw a man standing just inside. But unlike the thugs from before, this man looked perfectly suited to his environment. Whether because of his dark suit or stoic, distinguished manner, who could say?

"This is Fredrick," said Stallings.

Tracy stepped into the room and nodded.

"Hello," she said.

Frederick looked past her and raised his eyebrows at the lawyer. "Shall we begin?"

Stallings nodded.

"Please, Ms. Sterling. Have a seat."

He gestured to a specific chair on the far side of the conference table, and Tracy crossed the room and sat. After shutting the door, Stallings found a place near the back of the room and leaned against the wall.

"Go ahead, Frederick."

The distinguished-looking man nodded and held up a sheet of paper. Tracy watched with furrowed brows as the man cleared his throat and read aloud.

"Linda is 31 years old, single, outspoken, and very bright. She majored in philosophy in college and is deeply concerned with issues of social justice and discrimination.

"Based on what we know about Linda, which of the following two statements is more likely to be true? Choice A: Linda is a bank teller. Choice B: Linda is a bank teller and is active in the feminist movement."

"What?" asked Tracy.

The man peered at her over his glasses.

"Please answer the question."

Tracy looked past the man toward the lawyer, who stood with his arms crossed while leaning against the back wall.

"What is he talking about? she asked. "What does this have to do with anything?"

The lawyer looked at the man, who cleared his throat and frowned.

"Please, Ms. Sterling," said the man. "We have our reasons, and we believe they are justified. Now, if you'll just answer, we can move on. Would you like me to repeat the question?"

Tracy sighed audibly.

"Sure."

The man nodded and held the sheet of paper up to his face. He adjusted his glasses and read.

"Linda is 31 years old, single, outspoken, and very bright. She majored in philosophy in college and is deeply concerned with issues of social justice and discrimination.

"Based on what we know about Linda, which of the following two statements is more likely to be true? "Choice A: Linda is a bank teller. Choice B: Linda is a bank teller and is active in the feminist movement."

Tracy shook her head.

"A."

The man lowered the paper.

"And why did you choose option A?"

Tracy shrugged.

"Because it's the right answer."

The man looked back over his shoulder at Mr. Stallings, who raised his eyebrows.

"Please, Ms. Sterling," said Stallings. "Can you humor us with a deeper explanation?"

Tracy gave an exasperated sigh.

"It's an example of the representativeness heuristic," she said. "Intuitively, it seems like the second option would be right because of her apparent political leanings. But, statistically, the second statement is actually less likely because it's a subset of the first statement. So, it can't be more probable because it essentially represents a smaller sample that's already part of group A. In other words, if you choose A, you are choosing both B and countless other options, whereas choosing B limits your options and is, therefore, less likely."

Stallings turned toward the man and gave a nod.

"Let's move on to the second question."

The man held the paper up again and cleared his throat.

"Of the following two scenarios, which is more likely: A massive flood in the Midwest region of the United States kills 1,000

22

people. Or an earthquake in California causes a flood that kills 1,000 people."

He lowered the paper, and both men looked at Tracy, their faces pinched with interest.

"The first," she said flatly.

The man raised his eyebrows.

"And why did you choose the first option?"

Tracy shook her head.

"Because floods are more common than earthquakes. And the Midwest is a vast region of land. Whereas California is smaller, and earthquakes are relatively rare. And when they do occur, they rarely cause massive flooding. It's the representativeness heuristic again. The only reason anyone would choose the second option is because they associate earthquakes with California. Now, why am I answering these questions, and what in the hell is this all about?"

The man looked back at Mr. Stallings, who gave another little nod.

"One more, please."

Before Tracy could protest, the man held the paper up again and took in a breath.

"Steve is a 45-year-old man who is married with three children. He is well-educated and enjoys reading about political and social issues.

"Based on what we know about Steve, which statement is more likely to be true? Choice A: Steve is an accountant. Choice B: Steve is an accountant and a regular voter."

He lowered the paper and looked at Tracy.

"A," said Tracy. "And before you ask, it's the same reasoning as the first question."

Mr. Stallings stood up.

"Alright," he said. "That's enough, Fredrick. I think you can send our other candidates home."

The man nodded and turned toward the door. The lawyer watched him leave the room and then turned his eyes on Tracy.

"I'm very sorry for all that," he said. "The senator strongly values intelligent reasoning. And this is his rudimentary process to help weed out unfit candidates. Needless to say, you fared much better than your competition."

He approached and sat in the chair directly before her, his manner professional, face serious and nearly blank.

"Oh, it was a barrel of laughs," said Tracy. "Why don't you stop wasting time and tell me what this is all about?"

Mr. Stallings frowned.

"We're waiting for some other members of Senator Jenkin's team. They should be here shortly."

As if they had been listening just outside, the door opened, and two men entered. One, a short, middle-aged blonde man with distinguished good looks. The other, a tall, thin man with an appraising glare.

"This is Thomas," said the lawyer as he gestured toward the blonde man. "He's the senator's campaign manager."

Tracy nodded to the man.

"Nice to meet you," she said.

"Yes," said Thomas. "You, too."

Tracy's eyes moved to the tall, bald man, who stood straight with his hands folded at his waist.

"And who is this?" she asked.

Stallings turned to the man.

"This is Emmerich," said the lawyer. "He is part of the senator's security team."

Tracy assessed the tall man with a quick but thorough glance. His pale skin wrapped tightly around his sharp, angular face, giving it a harsh, skull-like appearance. And deep within that skull, his eyes burned in a vivid, unsettling way, as if he were a reptile wrapped in man flesh.

Tracy gave the thin man a nod.

"Shouldn't the senator's security man be with the senator?"

Emmerich stood quietly, while Thomas and Stallings exchanged glances.

"He's not that kind of security man," said the lawyer.

Tracy nodded.

"Ok."

Thomas looked at Tracy and smiled.

"We really appreciate you coming out tonight. I know this has been a bit of a pain. But the senator is particular about a lot of things. So, we do as we must."

Tracy sighed.

"It's fine," she said. "How about we get on with it, though?"

The campaign manager nodded.

"Sure," he said. "Mr. Stallings will explain things."

He turned to the lawyer and nodded.

"Ok," said Stallings as he sat back down. "Before we get started, we need you to sign this."

He withdrew a document and slid it across the table.

"What is it?" asked Tracy.

"It's a non-disclosure agreement. A standard NDA that says you can't go telling the media or anyone else about what I tell you tonight."

Tracy looked at the document.

"This isn't necessary," she said. "I wouldn't be much of a private investigator if I blabbed about my clients' business."

Stallings shrugged.

"Nonetheless."

Tracy skimmed the document.

"Alright," she said. "But I want an advance."

The lawyer nodded.

"You'll get $5,000 just for being here tonight, whether you accept the job or not."

Tracy scratched her jaw thoughtfully.

"Alright," she said.

They all watched as she signed the document.

"Now, can we get started?"

The lawyer took the NDA and nodded.

"Sure."

He passed the document over his shoulder to Thomas, who took it and stepped back.

"Ok," said the lawyer. "Let me just dive into it. We believe that Senator Jenkins will become the target of a murder probe in the coming weeks."

Tracy raised her eyebrows.

"I see. And why do you think this?"

Stallings shrugged.

"I'm not really at liberty to say at this time. What I can tell you is that we're taking proactive steps to help clear his name before such an investigation were to become public. And this is where you come in."

"Ok," said Tracy. "But you can't tell me why you believe he will be a person of interest in this hypothetical murder case?

"I'm afraid not."

Tracy sat back in her chair.

"If you're wanting me to prove that Senator Jenkins is innocent of a potential crime, it will be very difficult without all the information."

The lawyer nodded.

"We understand that."

Tracy furrowed her brows.

"And yet you're still planning to withhold details."

Stallings nodded.

"I'm afraid so."

"Why?" asked Tracy.

"Simple," said the lawyer. "In the event that we're wrong, and this unfortunate situation never comes to pass, we'd prefer to keep certain sensitive information out of the media. As I'm sure you can understand, Senator Jenkins has many political rivals who would jump at the chance to sully his reputation."

Tracy rubbed her jaw.

"Right. Well, who is the victim? Can you tell me that much, at least?"

"Her name is Dana Brockers," said Stallings.

"And when was she killed?"

The lawyer firmed his mouth.

"Well, this is where things get complicated," he said. "Ms. Brockers is still alive. As far as we know, at least."

Tracy raised her eyebrows.

"I'm sorry?"

Stallings turned a palm upward.

"I know it all sounds strange, Ms. Sterling. But technically, there is no victim. At least not yet."

Tracy looked past him toward the two other men, but they just stared back blankly from their positions against the wall.

"Ok," she said. "But you believe that this Dana Brockers will be killed at some point?"

"We have reason to think so. Yes."

Tracy shrugged.

"Why?"

"Again," said Stallings, "that's privileged information at this point. I'm sorry."

Tracy gave an exasperated sigh.

"Listen, if you have reason to believe that someone will be murdered, I would advise you to contact the police. Failing to do so

26

could leave you and the senator vulnerable to prosecution. This is true whether the senator is directly involved or not."

The lawyer nodded.

"The senator has been advised of this."

"And?" asked Tracy.

The lawyer shrugged.

"It is his decision to keep the knowledge private at this time."

Tracy frowned.

"Look, Ms. Sterling," said Thomas. "Senator Jenkins is not a cold man. He's just not fully certain that Ms. Brockers is in danger. And should he report his suspicions, he will open himself up to a police inquiry which will include media coverage and attacks from political rivals."

Tracy nodded.

"I see. Well, what about a warning? Why not tell this Dana Brockers her life may be in danger?"

Stallings shrugged.

"It is the senator's opinion that such a warning would be ignored. And frankly, he has no interest in opening up communications with Ms. Brockers."

Tracy shook her head a little.

"Alright, well, who is this girl to the senator? What's the connection?"

"She's just a college student," said Stallings. "No one important. I mean, not in the political arena."

Tracy stared into the lawyer's eyes.

"Did the senator have an affair with her?"

Stallings frowned.

"That's a very blunt question."

"I'm sorry," said Tracy. "But In my experience, you don't get very far by beating around the bush."

Stallings nodded.

"Well, as I said, I'm not at liberty to get into specifics. But I will say that as far as I know, there's no evidence Senator Jenkins has been anything other than a faithful husband."

"You sure?" asked Tracy. "Because if he did have a relationship with this Brockers woman, it would explain a lot."

Stallings shrugged.

"I can't help you there. I'm sorry. I think you will have to dig deeper than that."

Tracy sat back in her chair and looked over all three men.

"Ok. Let's focus on this Brockers woman," she said. "Why would someone want to kill her? Does she have enemies?"

The lawyer shrugged again.

"I couldn't say."

Tracy glared at him.

"Because you don't know, or you literally aren't allowed to say."

"I don't know," said Stallings. "But even if I did, I wouldn't be able to talk about it.

Tracy sighed.

"Alright, let me see if I have this straight. You want me to follow this woman and wait for someone to kill her? Doesn't that sound strange to you?"

The lawyer nodded.

"I can certainly see why you would feel that way. But this is the job. I know it's not perfect. But we have sound reasons for being discreet. And since we're not making things easy, the senator has instructed us to make sure you are well compensated if you choose to accept the job."

"How well compensated?" asked Tracy.

Mr. Stallings reached into his sportcoat and removed an envelope. He placed it flat against the table and slid it to Tracy, who immediately snatched it up. While the men watched, she removed a small slip of paper and read quietly to herself.

"This is a lot of money," she said.

Stallings nodded.

"This is a very important matter to the senator and his supporters. We're prepared to advance you with half that amount up front the second you agree to take this case."

Tracy glanced up at him, and then her eyes settled back on the paper.

"Alright," she said. "Let's say I agree to follow this woman. What if I witness an attack? I'm not going to just let her be killed. I will have to intervene."

The men exchanged looks, and all seemed to share the same frown. Tracy watched as Emmerich gave Stallings a nod, his hollow skull-like face sending shivers down her spine.

"Listen," said the lawyer at last. "We prefer that you refrain from interacting with Ms. Brockers. But if you can safely prevent an undesirable outcome, we'd encourage you to do so. That said, we have reason to believe that should a potential attack be thwarted, further attempts would be likely in the future."

Tracy looked at the paper one last time and then set it flat on the table.

"Can I be honest with you, Mr. Stallings?" she asked.

"Please," said the lawyer as he raised his eyebrows.

Tracy glanced at the other two men for a moment and then sat up in her chair.

"My intuition is telling me to decline this offer and go directly to the police," she said. "I understand that I have already signed your non-disclosure agreement. But I'm sure you know that it would not be enforceable if I were to reveal a crime."

Stallings firmed his mouth.

"Let me be clear," he said. "If you witness a crime during your investigation, we urge you to report it. But we must insist that you leave Senator Jenkins out of your statement to the media or police. Should we find that you have revealed your association with the senator unnecessarily, we will rigorously enforce the NDA in court, as we have many times before. I'm afraid this will be true whether you agree to take this case or walk away. Confidentiality is very important to us, Ms. Sterling. I cannot stress this enough."

Tracy sat back in her chair and sighed.

"This keeps sounding worse and worse."

Stallings watched her with an unsympathetic face, and just as he began to speak again, Thomas raised a hand to silence him.

"Listen," said the campaign manager. "I understand your apprehension, Ms. Sterling. I really do. But you have to understand; this is a delicate situation. The senator has a great many enemies. There are political rivals who want to unseat him. There are corporations and special interests who would profit greatly if many of his policies were overturned. He cannot afford a hit to his image. We need this resolved, and it needs to happen quietly."

Tracy looked up at him and narrowed her eyes.

"Why me?"

Thomas shrugged.

"The senator requested you personally."

"Why?" asked Tracy.

At last, Emmerich broke in.

"Because you have been on television," he said with a low, raspy voice.

Tracy forced herself to glare into his vivid eyes, which seemed to glitter within his deep skull sockets.

Stallings shrugged.

"He's right," said the lawyer. "You're here because of the media's obsession with the Alleyway Strangler case. The senator saw you on television and became enamored. Frankly, you were not our first choice. But the senator insisted. I mean that as no slight, Ms. Sterling. I just preferred a more experienced investigator. That said, you do have connections with the police, which might prove valuable."

Tracy put a hand to her chest.

"I'm flattered."

The lawyer shrugged.

"It's nothing personal," he said. "I'm old, and old people value experience. Maybe more than they should. I don't know. But truthfully, I have no reason to doubt your abilities. So, I'll try not to, at least as best I can. I can't speak for Emmerich, but I can speak for myself."

Tracy looked over at the security man, who was now studying his fingernails.

"Fair enough," said Tracy.

"So?" asked Stallings. "Do we have a deal?"

Tracy looked down at the paper one last time, her mind at war over an endless string of potential scenarios. But most of all, over the coming threat of making rent."

"Ok," she said. "But I'm not willing to be part of some coverup. And I won't withhold evidence of a crime from the police, even if it points to the senator. Non-disclosure agreement or not. Can you live with that?"

Stallings nodded.

"That's completely fair. We're confident you won't find anything linking the senator to this crime, if it ever occurs."

Tracy nodded.

"Ok, then," she said. "What can you share to help get me started?"

Emmerich approached and handed the lawyer a folder.

"Take this," said Stallings as he handed it over. It has all the basic details on Ms. Brockers. Where she lives, her college schedule and whatnot. I've had someone tailing her the past week. But my people are amateurs. So, I can't really give you any details on her routines."

Tracy looked through the folder.

"Well," she said. "It's a start.

Stallings produced some papers and spread them out on the table.

"If you'll just sign these documents regarding your payment, that will be the end of my involvement in the matter. Emmerich will be your point of contact going forward."

Tracy took a pen from his hand and signed the documents. When she was finished, the lawyer collected the papers. Then, he stuck out his hand and gave a polite smile.

"Good luck to you."

Tracy gave his hand a shake.

"Thanks."

The lawyer gave the campaign manager a nod, and then he and the security man both left the room.

"Well," Tracy said. "I certainly—"

"Listen," Thomas interrupted. "I'm sorry. I don't mean to be abrupt. But in a moment, Emmerich is going to enter and insist that he be your exclusive point of contact going forward. Now, there's nothing I can do about that. But I must ask that you also include me in your reports and keep our interactions secret from him. This is straight from the senator."

Tracy opened her mouth to respond, but the security man was already entering. With polite smiles, she and Thomas both greeted the tall, thin man, who responded with the same cold glare he'd worn the entire evening.

"Ms. Sterling," he said with a low whisper of a voice. "I understand you will need a degree of independence to carry out your duties. But it is my responsibility to ensure the safety of Senator Jenkins. So, I must insist that you coordinate your activities with me and my staff. And I will need weekly updates on your activities and any potential discoveries. You will report directly to me and no one else. Will that be a problem for you?"

Tracy glanced over to Thomas, who watched her with his eyebrows high on his forehead as if he were the one who had asked a question.

"No," she said. "It's not a problem. I mean, I will certainly do my best."

Emmerich stared down at her with an expressionless face, his eyes vibrant within the recesses of his bony, almost skeletal face.

31

"Please do."

He stepped forward and handed her a business card. Then, he turned toward Thomas and gave the slightest of nods before turning to leave the room.

When he was gone, Thomas let out a sigh.

"I'm sorry," he said. "I didn't mean to put you on the spot."

Tracy sat back in her chair and frowned, the gears in her head already turning to make sense of the encounter. Of the events of the whole night.

"You want to tell me anything else?" she asked.

Thomas shook his head.

"No. I really can't. I'm sorry. I'll just say that the senator is pretty freaked out right now. And he's not exactly sure who to trust. So, he wants to make sure he stays in the loop."

Tracy looked up at him thoughtfully.

"You don't trust Emmerich?"

Thomas shook his head.

"No, it's not like that. I mean, I hope not. Honestly, the senator is just not sure the security team will keep him fully informed, whether it's with the best of intentions or not. He just wants to make sure he knows what's going on. So, if you don't mind, please report to me as well. And let's just keep this to ourselves. Because Emmerich will not like it."

Tracy nodded.

"Yeah," she said. "I got that impression."

She stood up and stretched her back.

"Well," she said. "If you don't mind, I'd like to get started."

"Of course," said Thomas.

He led her out of the room and down the hallway, where she could plainly see the imprint of Emmerich's large narrow shoes in the plush carpet.

"Let me ask you something," she said to Thomas as they entered the elegant foyer.

"Sure."

He followed her outside, and they stood alone on the porch.

"Listen," she whispered. "This Emmerch, how far would he go to protect the senator's reputation?"

Thomas frowned at her.

"I get it," he said. "He's an icy guy. But I think you're on the wrong track. That said, you're the expert, so I'd encourage you to

32

follow your intuition. But do be careful. I mean, what I said about the senator having powerful enemies. Try to keep things as quiet as you can. We're just looking to keep the senator out of the headlines."

Tracy looked up at the mansion and nodded.

"I guess you don't get all this without stepping on a few toes."

Thomas looked at her and shrugged.

"Money is the mother's milk of politics, Ms. Sterling. It takes a lot of cash even to lose."

With that, he gave her a nod and went back inside, closing the big door behind him.

Chapter 3

Dana Brockers had a life carved from habit. She got up at the same time every day. She stopped every morning at the same coffee shop. She went to her classes using the same route. She ate at the same restaurants and shopped at the same stores. That made things simple for a private investigator. It also made things easy for a potential killer.

That wasn't the only thing that nagged at Tracy. There was also a growing sense that, despite Dana's predictable routine, something lurked beneath the surface, and the familiar was not as it seemed.

She'd followed the young woman for three days, and her habits were regular enough. At least during the light of day. And then, night claimed the city, and everything seemed to change.

Tracy expected nothing different on day four, as she sat in her car, parked at a discreet distance from Dana's apartment. It was morning, but the world seemed suspended between night and dawn, and Tracy yawned at the horizon until a hint of sun finally edged into view.

It would be another hour before Dana began her day. So, Tracy leaned her seat back and watched as the last of the stars vanished amid a blossoming sunrise of pink and orange.

When the sunlight finally spilled onto the pavement, Dana emerged from her apartment and scampered down a small flight of concrete steps. Tracy sat up and watched from afar, a pair of dark sunglasses hiding her eyes, which were webbed red by lack of sleep.

Dana's bouncy red hair glowed like a beacon in the morning light, making her easy to spot in a crowd. Tracy was thankful for that one little blessing in a case that already seemed riddled with needless encumbrances and missing puzzle parts.

With a little groan, she slipped out of her car and followed Dana across the road. The area was exceedingly walkable, and little stores lined the street as it cut a straight, easy path toward the bustling college campus. There were bagel shops, clothing boutiques and all the strategic trappings that might tempt a college student to surrender a portion of their student loan. But Dana Brockers didn't seem the type to make impulse purchases or unplanned excursions. And Tracy felt she could already predict the young woman's movements long before she made them.

Oblivious to her tail, the young woman hurried into a small crowd of pedestrians, her hair glowing like enchanted fire beneath the swelling morning sun. Without seeming to try, her beauty wielded its own gravity. And more than a few eyes appraised her tanned, athletic body, an alluring statement of vitality and youth.

As men stole glances at the attractive young woman, Tracy assessed each face for violent intent. But no one let their stare linger very long, and soon Dana had fled the street for a busy little coffee shop, where she ordered her usual latte with a polite, red-rimmed smile.

As the young woman traded words with the cashier, Tracy blended amid an eager little crowd, which had been lured in by the scent of fresh pastries and hot gourmet coffee.

When her order was up, Dana collected her drink and turned away from the counter, while Tracy feigned interest in a menu scribed on a chalkboard hanging against one far wall. Without paying any notice, Dana slipped out the door, and after a few ticks, Tracy did the same.

Onward they walked, Dana pushing forth toward the college campus with Tracy in tow about 100 feet behind. While the girl disappeared into the folds of academia, the crowd swelled around her, as students flowed toward their classes. Tracy pushed through, her shoulders banging other shoulders as she kept a sharp eye on the vivid torch that was Dana's red hair.

At last, they slipped through the crowd, and Tracy followed her into a large building of old red brick. Moving cautiously through the glass entryway, she watched Dana finish her coffee and toss it into a receptacle. Then, the young woman pushed through a door and took a seat amid nearly a hundred students in a vacuous lecture hall.

Tracy waited about a minute and then followed, her movements swift and drawing no attention as she slipped into the back row of the lecture hall. A few minutes passed, and then a hush fell over the crowd of students as an old bearded man shuffled onto the stage.

Bent by the decades, he cut a grumpy-looking figure, and everyone flinched as he approached a lectern and cleared his throat into the microphone. He paused and assessed the room with a sweeping glance. Then, he leaned toward the microphone and spoke in a deep, God-like voice.

"Did you know," he began, "that the CIA once attempted to use cats as espionage agents to gather intelligence on the Kremlin and Soviet embassies during the cold war?"

He glowered at the audience and waited.

"A veterinary specialist performed a 60-minute surgery to embed a microphone within the feline's ear canal, a miniature radio transmitter at the base of the animal's skull, and a slender wire woven into its coat. This enabled the cat to inconspicuously capture and broadcast audio from its environment."

He frowned down at his notes thoughtfully, while the students watched him with wrinkled brows.

"Unfortunately," he continued, "issues with the cat's distractions required another surgical intervention to address its hunger instincts. An ex-CIA operative by the name of Victor Marchetti estimated the project's expenses at around $20 million."

He raised his bushy gray eyebrows.

"The Acoustic Kitty initiative," he said. "A very real covert US spy program. Look it up with your Google or whatnot."

He adjusted his glasses and took in a deep breath.

"I would also ask if you are aware that from the 1500s all the way up to the 1900s, it was common practice for the average European to engage in acts of cannibalism as if it were no big deal at all."

He scanned the room and waited again.

"It may be difficult for your young minds to comprehend, but medicinal cannibalism in Europe was a very real thing. And not very long ago, people commonly consumed remedies made from human bones, fat and blood to address everyday ailments like headaches."

He frowned.

"I'm not talking about remote African tribes or ancient Incan societies. I'm speaking of England, Germany, France, Italy and even the US, all the way up to the early 1900s. During the seventeenth and eighteenth centuries, in fact, a thing called 'man's grease' saw a surge in popularity. Executioners would sell the fat of those they executed, which would be melted and stored in containers. Apothecaries marketed it as a treatment for pain, inflammation, rabies, joint issues and scarring."

His eyes seemed to twinkle as he swept them over the sea of young faces.

"The skin of the executed was also utilized for medicinal purposes," he said. "Expectant mothers actually wrapped the skin around their abdomens during childbirth to alleviate pain, while others wore it around their neck to prevent thyroid issues."

He shrugged.

"You did not know these things until this very moment because you are ignorant, despite what your parents may have told you. And believe me, this is but a fractional, infinitesimal example of the things your young minds do not know."

He frowned out at the crowd, and his mouth disappeared within his bushy beard.

"This quarter, I will attempt to assuage you of your ignorance of the world's bloody, disturbing history. And perhaps by consequence, you will have the slightest chance of not being helpless dupes for the rich and powerful liars who make the world."

As the professor continued his lecture, Tracy scanned the room, scrutinizing the other students, who seemed completely taken in by their teacher's dramatic introduction. Most of the room's inhabitants fixated on the man himself or their notebooks, while some seemed to drift toward the edge of sleep, while their little voice recorders saved up all the room's words for later.

But there was one young man, who caught Tracy's attention. He had a pale complexion and slim build, and he watched Dana over his dark-rimmed glasses, while she tilted her head to one side and dutifully scribbled notes.

Tracy watched him leer at the red-haired beauty from his discreet position, one row back, about five seats over. Again and again, he stole lingering glances, his knee bobbing nervously as he chewed the back of his pen.

With a slow hand, Tracy withdrew her phone and checked to make sure the flash was off on her camera. Then, she raised the device and snapped a few pictures of the young man, just as another student turned and pinned her with a pair of accusing eyes.

"What are you doing?" whispered the dark-haired young woman.

Tracy stopped and gave a polite smile.

"Getting some photos of the lecture," she said with a soft voice.

The young woman narrowed her eyes.

"It looked like you were taking pictures of the students."

This, she said with a louder voice that summoned the attention of two more students.

"Shh," one hissed.

The dark-haired girl spun toward the shushing sound.

"She's taking pictures of us," she said.

Tracy looked around to see that another half-dozen students had turned in their seats. She looked past them toward Dana who was still focused on the lecture — as was the professor, who hadn't yet noticed the disturbance at the rear of the audience.

"It's ok," Tracy whispered to all the curious faces. "I'm just getting some photos of the lecture."

This was enough to ward off some of the accusing stares. But the young dark-haired girl remained as before, her eyes looking Tracy up and down with self-righteous contempt.

"Aren't you a little old to be in this class?"

Tracy forced a pleasant smile.

"I work for one of the university's publications," she said. "I'm just getting some photos for an upcoming feature."

Unconvinced, the nosy young woman arched her eyebrows.

"Oh?" she asked. "Which publication?"

Tracy chewed her teeth.

"I'd be happy to discuss this with you after the lecture. But we're being rude. And I have a job to do."

With an uncertain frown, the student turned in her seat and folded her arms.

As the electricity ran from the air, Tracy started to release a little sigh, stopping abruptly when Dana turned in her seat and met her eye.

For the briefest moment, they stared at each other, Dana's brows furrowing over her vivid green eyes. Then, with a casual air, Tracy turned her attention to the professor and watched with feigned interest until Dana turned back around.

Silently cursing herself, Tracy glared at the back of the dark-haired student's head, her mind filling with fantasies of breaking the inquisitive girl's nose. With a few deep breaths, she tamed her temper and shook her head.

She hadn't been made, but the seeds of recognition had been sown. Now, she would have to use extra care to keep from being noticed going forward. Even an ill-timed glance would be enough to stir suspicion in Dana Brockers. The job had gotten harder, and she'd only been at it for just under four days.

To be safe, she slipped out of the lecture early and waited for the mob of students to flood the halls. After a while, Dana's burning red hair appeared amid the humanity, and Tracy followed her at a distance out of the building and into the warm spring sun.

The rest of the day progressed much as expected based on the previous three. As lunchtime rolled around, Dana met up with a stunning female friend at a cozy cafe near campus. Tracy couldn't help but marvel at this specimen, who was essentially a pale blond version of her tanned, red-headed counterpart.

By sheer luck, Tracy managed to snag a table outside, providing her with a clear view of the pair through a large window as they chatted over their meals.

While the two friends ate, Tracy took a few more discreet photos while scanning the surroundings for other watchers. There was an old couple sitting in silence as they repeatedly sunk their spoons into twin bowls of steaming soup. There were a pair of businessmen, barking about a recent financial report, their red, swollen faces advertising years of alcohol abuse. All in all, it was an ordinary crowd. So, Tracy drummed her fingers and waited until the two young women finished their meals and paid their bill.

As they left the restaurant, Dana and her friend walked arm in arm, their conversation a vibrant exchange of giggles and banter. Alone, they would have stopped traffic, but together, their beauty seemed amplified to ridiculous proportions. And people, made helpless by such power, gawked as they passed, both girls either oblivious or acclimated to the attention, their high-pitched laughter rising and falling as they ambled up the busy sidewalk.

After walking about a block, the pair entered a high-end clothing store, their steps in sync, laughter ringing like bells. Tracy followed from a distance, her presence a shadow on the periphery, as she slipped inside and found cover amid the racks of clothes. While the two young women shopped, she pretended to browse the merchandise, her fingers brushing against the expensive fabric as she feigned interest in the outrageously priced garments.

All the while, her trained eyes darted around the boutique in search of, what? A stalker from one of Dana's classes? A killer on the senator's payroll? In her mind, everything was on the table, especially with so little to go on.

Then, she noticed a man lingering outside the store window. From the corner of her eye, she watched as he cupped a hand over his eyes and peered through the glass. Without reacting, she plucked a dress from the rack and held it to her face, her eyes monitoring the man through the sheer, delicate fabric.

He was medium-built and around 30, and he wore a pair of sunglasses and a blue baseball cap. With what seemed like forced nonchalance, he stared through the glass at Dana and her friend. And then, for a brief but not insignificant moment, his head turned directly toward Tracy.

A little pang flickered within Tracy's chest as she felt the man's eyes fall upon her. With a casual air, she continued assessing the garment until she felt the heat of the man's stare cool. Then, she turned to watch him walk away down the sidewalk.

At the counter, Dana was purchasing a bright red dress, and Tracy noted that neither the young woman nor her friend seemed to flinch when the cashier reported the exorbitant price of the item. With a casual gesture, Dana simply reached into her purse and withdrew a tight bundle of neatly rolled cash.

Tracy cocked her head slightly as she watched the young woman strip away several one-hundred-dollar bills and pass them over. Then, Tracy retreated into a clothing rack as the cashier boxed up the item, and the two friends jauntily made their way out of the store.

"Can I help you with something?" asked the cashier.

Tracy held up a finger as she watched the two young women through the big window, her eyes darting about in search of the man in the baseball cap.

"Are you looking for something in particular?" the cashier continued.

Tracy said nothing, her eyes peering out the glass as Dana and her friend moved away from the store, the mysterious man nowhere in sight.

"Ma'am," said the cashier. "I'm afraid you will have to leave if you don't plan on purchasing anything."

Without responding, Tracy moved quickly across the store and slipped out the front door, while the cashier shook her head and returned to her work.

Outside, Tracy hurried to catch up as the two young women moved down the street. While she sifted through pedestrians, she glanced all around in a vain search for the mysterious man, who seemed to have vanished altogether. And after a while, she chalked her suspicions up to an increasing paranoia, fueled by the warnings from the senator's staff and the apparent obliviousness of Dana Brockers herself.

After a couple of blocks, the two young women turned a corner and walked down an intersection street. Tracy used the opportunity to close the gap, hurrying past other pedestrians as they browsed through store windows. Reaching the edge of the building, she turned and saw that both women were entering a jewelry store. When they disappeared inside, she made her way up the sidewalk and stopped at the edge of the storefront window. With a careful movement, she peered around the edge and cupped a hand to look within.

On the other side of the glass, Dana and her friend were grinning down at a display case, as a thin mustached man gestured toward the items within. At Dana's behest, the man withdrew a glittering diamond tennis bracelet and passed it to the redhead with care. The girl's eyes sparkled with delight as she slipped the piece onto her wrist. She held it up and admired her arm, where the large, scintillating gemstones flickered with a radiant fire to match that of her magnificent red hair.

While Tracy pondered the price tag of such an item, something caught her eye. With a casual air, she swallowed and moved back a few inches from the window. As she did, the sunlight caught the glass and returned her reflection, and with it, that of the man with the baseball cap, who was watching the jewelry store from across the street.

Without moving, Tracy continued to stare forward, her eyes studying the man's reflection as he watched the store. He had tried to conceal himself behind a stone pillar just outside a bank, but his sunglasses gave him away, their lenses glaring like beacons in the bright sunlight.

Tracy watched the man for a moment longer, and then she felt her heart jump as she adjusted her eyes to see that Dana and her friend had turned toward the storefront window.

With a calm movement, Tracy turned away and walked down the street, dissolving within a cluster of pedestrians as she approached the edge of the next block.

While she walked, Tracy tried in vain to get glimpses of the world behind her in the rearview mirrors of cars parked along the curb. And then, at last, she passed a large delivery truck with an oversized mirror that gave back much of the world in reverse.

To her dismay, she saw that the man had crossed to Dana's side of the road. But instead of pausing outside the jewelry store, he continued down the sidewalk in Tracy's direction as she moved further and further away from Dana and her friend.

A swirl of thoughts swam within Tracy's head as she continued to move down the street. Either she had become distracted by an implausible coincidence; or she, and not Dana Brockers, was the one being followed.

Her mind raced as she considered why anyone would put a tail on her. All the previous cases she'd worked over the last year. Anyone who might have a grievance against her. But after a while, she grew tired of pondering and decided the best tactic was her usual one: a blunt, direct approach.

With a casual, easy pace, she continued to the edge of a building and turned abruptly down a little alley that cut between a pair of two-story brick buildings. Once she disappeared around the corner, she trotted a few yards and then crouched behind a big dumpster filled with cardboard boxes and packing material.

There she waited, her breath slow and easy as she slipped her pistol from the holster inside her jacket. She waited in silence, her ears straining to listen over the faint sound of traffic murmuring out on the main road.

Seconds turned to minutes before she finally heard the crunch of bad pavement beneath a pair of heavy shoes. As adrenaline flooded her veins, she held her breath and waited while the footsteps grew louder. And then just as the man hurried past the dumpster, she reached a hand out and tripped him at the ankle.

Flailing wildly, the man sprawled forward and collided with the ground, his hat and sunglasses flying free as his face slapped the alleyway floor.

Without hesitating, Tracy raced forward and positioned herself at his side. As he pushed himself upward, she drove the sharp toe of her shoe into his lower ribs, and the man cried out as he collapsed back onto his stomach. He cursed and flipped over, his face seized by rage and then fear as he looked up at the business end of Tracy's pistol.

"Can I help you with something?" she asked with a calm, flat voice.

The man raised his hands in surrender, his bloody mouth stammering gibberish as he cowered away from her.

"Slow down," said Tracy.

The man took a breath and shook his head.

"Please," he said. "Put the gun down."

Tracy narrowed her eyes.

"I'd like to ask you a couple of questions first. Let's start with why you're following me."

The man swallowed and shook his head.

"I can't."

Tracy stepped closer to the man and aimed the gun between his open legs.

"Really?"

The man forced a mocking smile which belied the fear in his watering eyes.

"Come on," he said. "You're not gonna shoot me. You were a cop."

She shrugged.

"I was a cop. I'm not anymore."

He opened his mouth to speak, but his words transformed into a shriek as she drove the toe of her shoe into his testicles. Almost at once, the man's face turned bright red as the pain radiated into his abdomen. He coughed and moaned as he rolled over and clutched his manhood.

Tracy stepped back and waited, her pistol still aiming at the man, who vomited onto the street and then gasped mutely like a fish tossed upon land.

"You ready to answer my questions?" asked Tracy as the man's breathing slowed.

43

He turned over and looked at her, his face now pallid and marred by flecks of vomit.

"Who are you?" she asked. "And why are you following me?"

The man gasped a little and raised up to a sitting position.

"I work for the senator's security detail," he said. "Emmerich told me to keep an eye on you."

Tracy frowned at his words.

"Why?" she asked.

He shrugged.

"He doesn't tell me why. He just tells me what to do."

Tracy shook her head and let out a sigh.

"Well," she said. "You can tell him I work alone. So, that means you get to take the rest of the day off."

She holstered her weapon before reaching into her jacket to withdraw a little handkerchief.

"Here," she said as she tossed it to him. "Sorry about your balls."

With that, she turned and walked out of the alley, the man watching her with genuine fear as she rounded the corner.

By the time she made it back to the jewelry store, Dana and her friend were long gone. She cursed inwardly as she hurried back to her car. It was Thursday, and that meant the young woman had only the one morning class. The day was young, and there was no way to know where Dana had gone or what she might be doing. At least not until sundown.

When Tracy reached her car, she slipped inside and stared at Dana's apartment. The day had been anything but smooth. But if it ended like the last three, she knew where to pick up the young woman's trail.

The night would end at Dougie's, a seedy gentlemen's club on the south side of the city. As long as no one killed Dana until then, everything would be alright. She started her car and pulled away, her mind at war with intrusive thoughts of Dana splayed out in a gutter with her throat cut and bright red blood spilling into her flaming red hair.

Chapter 4

Tony shuffled up the sidewalk and assessed the big parking lot, his hand rubbing his chin as he looked all around. The blacktop was warped, and tall weeds poked out from tiny fissures within the decaying surface. He looked down and snorted the air. The dark, crumbling aggregate smelled bitter as it baked beneath the sun. He sniffed again and gave a little smile.

It reminded him of summer, that stench. The long-lost summers of his youth. A simpler time when he would frequent the state fair with the other scammers and pickpockets — most of whom had gone on to serve at least five to ten in state prison.

Not Tony, though. He was luck's very child. And his ability to skirt the law inspired the kind of confidence you needed in this profession. He nodded at the thought as if to agree with himself. Then, he crossed into the parking lot and looked around.

The old hardware store loomed on the far side of the lot, its windows boarded up, colorful graffiti tattooing the warped gray wood. That business had closed years ago, but people still used to the lot. After all, who could pass up free parking in a city like this? And yet, by Tony's count, the lot was only about 70 percent full on this late afternoon. A rare occurrence, and a fortunate one from his perspective. He nodded in agreement to this thought as well. Then, he turned toward the entrance and unfolded his cheap little lawn chair.

He sat and leaned back, the chair whining under the meager stress of his small body. Within minutes, a car pulled up to the entrance, the driver looking confused as Tony jumped up to stand in his way.

"How you doin today, sir?" he asked.

The driver was a professional-looking, middle-aged man with a neatly parted haircut. He assessed Tony with a curling lip.

"I'm fine," he said. "Now, please, if you don't mind, can you step aside? I'm in a hurry."

Tony ran a hand over his slicked-back hair and gave an affable grin.

"I'd be happy to," he said. "I just need $20 from you first."

The man's face turned sour.

"What?"

Tony raised his eyebrows.

"Cash only, I'm afraid. We aren't equipped to take plastic yet. Maybe next week. They're still getting their ducks in a row."

The man shook his head.

"What in the hell are you talking about?"

"Parking," said Tony. "It's $20 for this lot. Covers the whole day. Pretty sweet deal if you ask me."

The man gave a stunned look.

"But this lot has always been free."

Tony shook his head.

"Well, sir. That may have been the case before. But the lot was recently purchased by a real estate investment company. And what was true before, well, it ain't no more."

The man started to protest, but another car had pulled in behind him.

"Please, sir," said Tony. "Either pay the fee or move on. I've got other interested parties."

With unconcealed rage, the man plunged his hand into his jacket pocket and withdrew a roll of bills. Tony felt his tongue involuntarily swab his lips as he eyed the wad of cash.

"Here," said the man as he shoved over a twenty-dollar bill."

Tony plucked the money from his hand and jammed it into his pocket.

"Thank you, sir," he said as he moved out of the way.

The man drove into the lot and made way for the next driver, who seemed equally dismayed by the strange little man blocking his path.

About two hours later, the lot was nearly full, and Tony's pockets were bulging with cash. He didn't dare count his score — not out in the open like this. But he figured it was only half of what he needed. And now there were only a handful of spaces left. He cursed at himself for arriving late to the scene. But it had been a long night, and he was still nursing a hangover even as the failing sun reddened the horizon.

As he rubbed his temples, Tony felt his phone vibrate within his pocket. With a quick hand, he withdrew the device and eyed the caller. He pinched his eyebrows together and then put the phone to his ear.

"Ms. Sterling," he said. "What can I do you for?"

"I've got a little job for you," said Tracy.

Tony eyed the lot and frowned.

"What's it pay?"

"Don't you want to know what it is?" asked Tracy.

"Sure," he said.

"It's a simple thing. Nothing dangerous. I just need you to watch someone for a few hours."

Tony raised his eyebrows.

"And who might that be?"

"A college-aged girl I've been tailing. She's moonlighting at a local strip club. I imagine she's a waitress there or possibly even a dancer. I would stick out like a sore thumb in this place. So, I need someone of—" she paused for a moment—"your caliber."

Tony looked at the lot and stood up.

"Ma'am, you had me at college-aged girl."

Tracy sighed through the phone.

"Just meet me at Dougie's at 10 tonight."

Tony froze.

"Did you say Dougie's?"

That's right," said Tracy. "Why? Is that a problem?"

Tony frowned into the phone.

"Boy you really are outside the loop," he said. "Dougie's isn't some ordinary strip joint. It's a dangerous place run by a dangerous man. Some of the shit that goes on there would make me blush, and that's saying something."

Tracy sighed.

"Fantastic."

It was quiet for a moment.

"Are you known there?" asked Tracy.

Tony shrugged.

"It depends on the night's clientele," he said. "But don't worry. I can keep a low profile anywhere. But for a place like this, I'm gonna have to charge a premium."

"How much?" asked Tracy with a sharp voice.

"Well," said Tony. "Some of my associates are involved in a big play, and I need some cash for a buy-in."

"You mean these men are running a con on some rich mark?" asked Tracy.

Tony smiled.

"Somethin like that."

Tracy sighed again.

"How much is your buy-in?"

"About five grand."

"Five grand?" said Tracy. "Or about five grand?"

"Five grand," said Tony.

"How short are you?" asked Tracy.

Tony ran a hand over the bulge in his pocket.

"Three thousand."

It was quiet for a moment.

"Alright," said Tony. "Let's call it two thousand."

Tracy sighed one last time.

"Fine," she said. "I'll cover the rest of your buy-in. But you'll have to put in for more than one night. I want you here every night until I'm through with this case. If it runs long, I'll compensate you. Deal?"

Tony grinned.

"Sure thing. What's this girl's name?"

"Just meet me in the parking lot at Dougie's tonight at ten. I'll give you what you need then."

"Whatever you say," said Tony.

The phone clicked quiet, and Tony slipped it into his pocket. Then, he stood up and stretched his back. As he bent to fold his chair, a car pulled into the lot and idled.

"How much for parking?" asked a man through his open window.

Tony gathered up his chair and looked back at the lot.

"It's free," he said as he walked away.

Tracy sat in her car in the parking lot outside Dougie's, her eyes darting about in search of Tony, as she fantasized ways to beat him black and blue. It was 11 p.m., and he was still nowhere in sight, and she cursed herself for placing even a fraction of faith in a man like him.

She tapped her steering wheel with a nervous hand and looked around. A small sea of cars littered the unpainted lot, which led to an old brick building, where a neon sign said in big blistering-red letters, "Girls, Girls, Girls." Somewhere in the darkness, there was another sign that said "Dougie's," but that seemed secondary enough to warrant no light at all.

It was all about the girls, Tracy thought. And one of them was named Dana Brockers, who'd been inside moving about her business unobserved for at least an hour. She shook her head and cursed Tony's name, just as he appeared from the blackness.

She watched as he approached, his hands in his pockets as he squinted into the dark parking lot. The place was packed, and Tracy blended nicely amid the other vehicles, her face lost in the shadows which concealed the rage in her eyes.

After watching him search in vain for several minutes, she lowered her window and gave a sharp whistle. He flinched as if someone had fired a rifle. Then, he turned and trotted over, his face split into a slimy grin as he approached.

"Hey," he said.

"Get the fuck inside," said Tracy.

Tony looked hurt as he popped open the door and slid into the passenger seat.

"What's the problem?" he asked with what seemed like genuine interest.

"The problem is you're late."

His face looked doubtful.

"You said 10:30."

Tracy narrowed her eyes.

"I said 10."

He frowned at her.

"You sure?"

"Yes, I'm fucking sure!" she hissed. "And even if I had said 10:30, you'd still be a half-hour late."

Tony shrugged.

"My mistake."

Tracy put a hand to her forehead and sucked in a few calming breaths.

"Damn," said Tony as he looked up at the club entrance. "This place is hopping. They must have some real talent on stage tonight."

Tracy glared at him.

"That's none of your concern," she said. "You're here to keep a close eye on someone. I don't want you losing sight of this girl because some blonde jiggles her tits at you."

Tony shrugged.

"Of course," he said with a reassuring smile. "I'm a professional, after all."

Tracy flexed her jaw.

"So," said Tony. "Who is this girl anyway?"

"I told you before," said Tracy. "She's a college-aged girl I've been tailing for a client. Most of her days seem to end here. I guess she's a waitress or maybe a dancer. I don't know because if I go in there, I won't blend in very well."

Tony chuckled.

"I don't know," he said. "Don't sell yourself short. You've got a look."

She flashed her teeth, and he cowered a little.

"I mean among the clientele," she said.

Tony nodded.

"Sure. I get it." He shrugged. "So, who's your client? Some pervert who's got a thing for this girl? What's her name anyway?"

Tracy shook her head.

"I don't work for perverts. And the client is confidential. Your only concern is keeping an eye on this girl. Her name is Dana Brockers."

Tony turned away and looked at the entrance to the club, the flickering neon lights reflecting in his pale eyes.

"Dana Brockers," he repeated.

"Yes," said Tracy. "Now, this is important, so pay attention."

He turned and looked at her with his most serious face.

"I have good reason to believe she's in danger," said Tracy. "My client suspects someone may make an attempt on her life. If something like that occurs, if she seems to be in any danger at all, you text or call me immediately."

Tony furrowed his eyebrows.

"And then what?" he asked. "You come storming in with your guns blazing?" He shook his head. "Do you know who runs this joint?"

Tracy flexed her jaw.

"Vincent Costa."

Tony raised his eyebrows.

"Oh, so you do know," he said. "Because you were acting like you didn't. Do you also know that he runs drugs in and out of the city? And do you also know that he is connected to some of the most dangerous organized criminals on the whole East Coast?"

Tracy shook her head.

"None of that matters," she said. "I'm not asking you to take him down. Just keep an eye on this girl. I don't anticipate anything happening to her here."

Tony gave a mocking shrug.

"Oh, you don't anticipate. I see." He pointed toward the club, where an enormous bouncer was turning away a staggering drunk. "People die in this place all the time."

Tracy lowered her eyebrows.

"All the time?"

Tony shrugged.

"Well, maybe not all the time, but enough for my taste."

He shook his head.

"Listen," he said. "I'll take your money and I'll go in there to keep an eye on this girl. But the first sign of something violent, and I'm out the door." He shrugged again. "I ain't no hero."

Tracy shook her head.

"Fine," she said. "Just watch her. Let me know if she has any interactions with someone suspicious. Anyone who might mean her harm. Try to find out who they are, so I can look into them."

Tony shook his head.

"This ain't no run-of-the-mill job," he said. "You're asking me to do more than just watch."

She withdrew a wad of cash and held it so it could not be missed.

"Well, that's the job," she said. "Can you handle it or not?"

He looked at the cash and rubbed his jaw, his eyes flaring a little as his mind worked.

"Yeah," he said. "I can handle it."

He reached out for the cash, and she pulled it away.

"Then, handle it," she said as she put the money back into her pocket.

He looked at the cash a little longer. And then, he gave a nod and stepped out of the car. Tracy watched as he hurried to the front of the club and took a place at the back of the line. When it was his turn to stand before the bouncer, he grinned up at the huge man, who eyed him with a wrinkled lip, as if he were laying eyes on some kind of huge grotesque insect. Then, he gestured Tony inside, and Tracy was left to imagine the happenings within.

Time passed, as she sat and watched from the shadows. Men came and went, their faces eager and hard and coveting what lay within. All the while, the club's neon lights sputtered and strobed, casting garish colors against the black parking lot.

She glanced around the lot to ensure her solitude. And then her eyes settled at the entrance of the club. There, the massive bouncer stood sentinel, a hulking silhouette before all the colorful luminescence.

As he dealt with the slow stream of horny men, the monster's broad shoulders rippled beneath his jacket, as if the muscles and sinews were straining to be unleashed. This was not lost on the men who approached, and each seemed to shrink in his presence, their bravado fading like smoke in the wind.

Tracy tapped her steering wheel and sat in silence as the scene played out before her, a spectacle both mundane and yet charged with the potential for violence. But the bouncer's dominance proved absolute, so she yawned and stretched back in her seat, her stomach rumbling as she collected a bag of mixed nuts from the glove box.

Without taking her eyes from the club, she brought the bag to her lips and let a few almonds tumble into her mouth. She watched the entrance, her eyes resisting the siren song of her thermos on the passenger floorboard.

She'd learned fast that being a PI meant holding in piss for hours at a time, and that was a battle she didn't want to wage on this particular evening. So, she chewed dryly and swallowed hard while the bouncer peopled the club for the next hour.

As the night wore on, the steady rhythm of entering and exiting patrons marked the passage of time, each face a fleeting portrait of desire and escape. And then, at last, the mundane gave way to the inevitable as a loud inebriate attempted to make his way inside.

Tracy sat up and watched as the bouncer straightened, his body seeming to grow in size as the man's shrill voice broke the night's spell. The drunkard's swagger had become an unsteady stumble, but the alcohol in his veins lent him the requisite insanity to challenge the keeper of the club.

The giant, accustomed to the desperation and unruliness of these sorts of men, moved swiftly. There was no negotiation or sympathy in his demeanor. With violent contempt, he collected the man in his huge hands and hoisted him from the ground as if he weighed nothing more than a feather. The drunk man's limbs flailed wildly, as he made a futile attempt to regain control over his own body. But as quickly as the altercation had begun, it ended, the bouncer tossing the man onto the cold concrete, where his body crumpled like a discarded bag of trash.

Tracy watched as the drunk's friends peeled him from the parking lot and dragged him away. Then, she sat back in her seat and tossed a few more nuts into her mouth.

Another hour passed, and Tracy felt the slow hand of time in her aching legs and back. The minutes seemed to drag their feet like petulant children, each second a grueling ordeal as she struggled to get the blood flowing in her limbs amid the cramped confines of her car.

Another hour passed with no distractions from the maddening stillness of her mind, which filled with insane imaginings of what must be going on inside the club.

With a sigh, she slumped in her seat, while the flickering neon light cast eerie shadows across her face, reflecting her boredom and growing fatigue.

And then, a fresh commotion snapped her from a sleepy trance.

She narrowed her eyes and watched, her ears straining to make sense of the growing noise just inside the club. The bouncer moved away from the line of men and turned toward the door, just as it burst open and slammed against his shoulder.

With a flinch, the big man moved aside as Tony flew by and skidded face-first on the concrete.

"Oh, shit," said Tracy as she straightened in her seat.

The tiny crowd watched as Tony scrambled forward on his knees, his face bloody and stricken by fear. And then, came another man, big in his own right, and clearly eager to finish whatever had started within the club's interior.

Before the bouncer could intervene, the man had exited the club and set upon Tony, his hands clenched into big fists as he made his way toward the shrieking little man.

"Stop!" cried the bouncer, but the man didn't seem to hear.

Instead, he drove his shoe into Tony and flipped him over onto his back. Now, the bouncer had fled his post and was bearing down on the man. With a violent jolt, he placed a great hand on the man's shoulder and turned him so they were face to face. But before he could speak, the man jabbed him in the throat with a lightning-quick fist.

The small line of men gave a collective gasp as the bouncer stumbled backward, his eyes bulging as he clutched his throat. Without hesitating, the man turned away from the bouncer and looked down at Tony, who was now on his knees. As the man approached, Tony clasped his hands together and pleaded for mercy, his face a bloody ruin as he slobbered and cried. And then, he stuck a hand out and pointed toward Tracy, who felt a cold chill run down her spine.

The man turned away from Tony and looked directly at her car, his body heaving with big breaths, face lost to the shadows.

"Oh, shit," whispered Tracy as she reached for her pistol.

Without speaking, the man jabbed Tony in the face, and the small man collapsed to the ground. Then, while the bouncer and crowd watched, the man gathered Tony by the back of his shirt and lifted him like a suitcase.

Tracy watched as the man approached, Tony dangling from one big arm. With every step, she clutched her gun, her heart throbbing as the dark figure moved deliberately in her direction. And then, she let out a breath as the neon light illuminated the man's features.

"Oh, shit," she whispered as Jimmy Hunter stopped in front of her car.

He looked at her through the windshield, his face vague as ever.

"This belong to you?" he asked.

She watched as he dropped Tony to the ground and moved to her side of the car. She swallowed as he gestured for her to lower her window.

"What the hell are you doing here?" he asked. "And why in God's name are you working with this piece of filth?"

Tracy glanced over at Tony, who seemed to be drifting between the realms of blissful unconsciousness and agonizing reality. Then, her eyes flicked over to the bouncer, who was now standing with two of the club's burly security men, their hard eyes looking her way with what seemed like violent intent.

"Let me call you later," she said. "I think we'd better get out of here while we can."

Jimmy stared down at her with his usual blank expression.

"Do you mind giving me a hand with him?" asked Tracy as she gestured toward Tony.

Jimmy shook his head and moved toward the bleeding man, who was now conscious enough to cower at the sight of his abuser. With a swift motion, he gave Tony one final kick and then stepped back as the whimpering man vomited onto the pavement.

Tracy watched as Jimmy snagged Tony by the collar and dragged him to her car. With a hard jerk, he opened the door and tossed the bloody man into the passenger seat.

Tracy grimaced as the smell of blood and vomit invaded the vehicle.

"Thanks for that," she said dryly, as Jimmy slammed the door.

"No problem," he said.

Tracy stifled a gag as she started her car.

"You'd probably better leave off too," she said to Jimmy through the window. "Those guys are admiring your handiwork."

Jimmy turned and spat on the concrete.

"Just worry about yourself."

With that, he turned and walked away. Tracy lowered her eyebrows and watched for a few seconds longer. But then Tony vomited again, so she cursed him and pulled away, leaving Dana Brockers and the mysteries of Dougie's behind her.

Out on the road, Tony was beginning to regain his senses, and this led to a series of low agonizing moans. Tracy eyed his swelling face as she leaned away to breathe the fresh air gushing through her open window.

"I'm going to drop you off at the hospital," she said. "I've got to get back before Dana leaves the club."

Tony whimpered and coughed.

"No," he gasped as he tried to sit up in his seat. "No hospital."

55

She looked at his broken nose and grimaced at the blood smears on her passenger seat.

"Why not?" she asked. "You've probably got some busted ribs. And you need to get that nose set, or you'll be uglier than you already are."

He coughed again and swallowed something vile.

"No," he gasped. "They'll report it. And then I'll have to deal with the cops. I got a record. I can't get caught up with cops right now. I'll set the nose myself."

She shook her head in disgust and stared out at the coming road.

"What the hell did you do to get Jimmy that worked up?"

Tony shrugged and then shrieked a little from the pain.

"He thinks I conned him out of some money a few months back."

Tracy looked over at him.

"Did you?"

He almost shrugged again but thought better of it.

"It depends on how you look at it."

Tracy sighed and looked back at the road.

"I can't think of a worse person to try to con."

Tony put a hand to his mouth and wiggled a loose tooth.

"Yeah," he said.

They drove for a few minutes longer before pulling before a small apartment building that looked more like a drug den than an actual residence.

"This is the place," said Tony.

Tracy bent to look out through the passenger window. Six stories high, the aged structure loomed at the end of the desolate street. Weathered and stained, its brick exterior was a patchwork of crumbling masonry and graffiti-covered walls. The building's fire escapes, a tangled mess of rusted metal, groaned and shifted under the weight of their own deterioration. The surrounding neighborhood, once vibrant and bustling, had long since succumbed to the same fate. This was a place where hope and happiness had been forgotten, replaced by an oppressive air of despair.

"You're living here?"

He shrugged.

"Just for a little while. I've got a big score coming up. Then, I'm skipping town."

56

She looked at him.

"You're going to do your little con job with that face."

He shrugged again and grimaced.

"Believe me, it ain't little. Anyway, it might even help, believe it or not."

She shook her head as he opened the door and struggled to step outside.

"Thanks," he said as he looked back. "Sorry about the mess."

She nodded.

"Sure," she said as she looked him up and down. "No offense, but I think this may be the last time we work together."

He gave a little nod.

"I understand."

He sucked at the loose tooth and spat a red glob onto the filthy sidewalk.

"Can I give you some advice though?" he asked.

"Sure," she said. "Why not?"

He furrowed his brows.

"You shouldn't go back to that place. Not tonight. Not ever."

"Why's that?" she asked.

He firmed his ruined mouth, which had already swollen to twice its original size.

"Look," he said. "I like you. I really do. You're a tough one, no doubt about that. I wouldn't want to be on your bad side. But even still, you ain't cut out for that kind of world. The men that run that place are harder than you. Harder than me. That place is dangerous. You'd better believe it. Even for ex-cops. Especially for ex-cops."

She nodded.

"I appreciate the advice."

He nodded.

"Sure," he said as he turned and limped away. "See you around."

Without hesitating, Tracy put the car in drive and turned back toward Dougie's. If she hurried, she could pick up Dana's trail before the girl left work and made her way home. She glanced at the clock and cursed silently as she jammed her foot against the accelerator.

Out on the road, the city lights twinkled in the gloomy night. Off in the distance, tall buildings loomed out of the darkness and soared upward into a black sky that was streaked with smoke from refineries and street traffic, a ceaseless river of metal even at this late hour.

Before Tracy's tired eyes, the city seemed to go on forever, as if it truly had no end. And as she raced back toward the gentlemen's club, she felt a strange sense of panic amid all the ceaseless sprawl.

Shaking these thoughts away, she raced back toward the gentlemen's club, arriving just minutes after the end of Dana's shift. But as she neared the lot, a sense of relief spread through her body when she saw Dana's car.

Slowing her vehicle, Tracy killed her headlights and eased into the back of the parking lot, coming to a halt several yards behind Dana's car.

Amid the weak light of a tall, parking lot lamp, she could see into the vehicle's back window well enough to tell that the young woman was already inside, her lush red hair spilling over the sides of the headrest.

Tracy let out a deep breath and shook her head. Despite a night of amateurish mishaps, she hadn't lost her after all. And though the happenings within the club remained mysterious, the night was not a total loss.

Tracy idled her car at a careful distance, her fingers tapping the steering wheel as she waited for Dana to start her car and make her way home. But as seconds turned to minutes, impatience began to prick at her mind, and her heart picked up some as she studied the young woman for movements.

After 20 minutes, Dana remained as before, the car still, engine silent, even as the lot began emptying around her.

Tracy sat up in her seat and chewed her teeth. Was she on the phone? Was she getting high? Had she inexplicably fallen asleep after a long night of work?

She felt her hand curl involuntarily around her door handle and stopped before pulling it open. If she approached Dana now, her cover would be blown for sure. So, she resettled in her seat and tapped her foot against the floorboard.

More and more vehicles fled the lot, as the last of the customers staggered out of the building. A heavily inebriated man dropped his pants and urinated for all to see, while another vomited a few feet away. Then, they both crawled into a truck, which lurched and swerved as they drove away into the night.

Another 20 minutes passed, the lot was mostly empty, and Dana remained as before, her head pointed forward, as if she were sleeping or lost in a ticklish set of thoughts.

At last, Tracy cursed and opened her door. Carefully and quietly, she stepped out onto the blacktop and unholstered her pistol. Slowly she crept forward, bits of loose gravel crunching beneath her shoes as she approached the vehicle from behind.

Soon, she was close enough to get a look in the side mirror, where she caught a glimpse of Dana's green eyes, wide and vacant, staring upward with fear and shock.

Tracy rushed forward and looked inside the car.

"Oh, no," she whispered as her eyes took in the ghastly scene.

The dashboard was spattered red, like some sick mural painted by a madman's hand. Tracy put a hand over her mouth as her eyes travelled to Dana's neck, where a deep gash ran from ear to ear. The wound had all but severed the young woman's head from her body, spilling rivers of dark blood across her pale white skin.

Instinctually, Tracy raised her gun and spun around, her eyes peering into the uninhabited darkness. Then, she turned back toward the car and put a hand over her mouth as she looked upon Dana's colorless face. Wide and stargazing, the young woman's once-vibrant green eyes seemed muted and soulless. Her hair, once touched by fire, seemed diminished and dull, as if its essence had seeped out the great wound along her butchered neck.

Off in the distance, highway noises ebbed and flowed. Somewhere close by, a dog barked in the night.

Tracy shook her head and firmed her mouth.

"I'm so sorry," she whispered.

She stared at the young woman a while longer, her eyes sweeping the body for any visible clues. But there was nothing much to see. So, she walked away and sniffled a little before withdrawing her phone to call the police.

Chapter 5

Tracy sat alone in the cold, stark interrogation room amid the unsettling hum of fluorescent lights. The place hadn't changed a bit since her last visit. But there was no comfort in that. Things did not feel familiar in the least. And it didn't take long to realize there was a big difference on this side of the table.

She looked around and shifted in her seat, a squeak detonating amid the hollow silence as she looked around the room. The walls, sterile and white, seemed to press inward, shutting out the warm, comforting exterior world. The air, tinged with the acrid scent of stale cigarettes and sweaty desperation, clung to her lungs with every suffocating breath.

The linoleum floor, speckled with gray and black, seemed to vibrate with the ghostly energy of past interrogations. The scuffs underfoot, a testament to the violent convergence of fear and truth. The table, a cruel slab of metal, bore the weight of countless secrets and hard-won confessions. Tracy ran a hand over the chilly steel, her eyes falling on the dent from the time Bradley slammed a drug dealer's head against it, while the chief yawned as he watched from the other room.

She took in a slow, deep breath and looked over at the one-way mirror. Someone on the other side looked back, but their identity remained shrouded by the hazy glass. She stared directly into her own reflection and forced a yawn, a performative act that belied the anxiety running like icy streams within her chest.

The glint of the metal doorknob caught her eye as it began to turn. She straightened in her chair and threw her shoulders back. Then, she looked up and gave a little smile.

"Hello, Tracy," said John as he stepped into the room.

She sat back in her seat and watched him, a weary figure that looked overburdened by the weight of his job.

"They moved you to homicide?"

He shrugged and took a seat at the table.

"Well, we were a little short-handed for a while. So, I figured, what the hell?"

Tracy nodded as he set a folder down on the table.

"It suits you. You've got a mind for it."

He gave a little nod.

"The pay is better, at least."

It was quiet for a moment as he appraised her with a wary eye.

"So," she said. "How have you been?"

He frowned at her.

"Tracy, what were you doing at this crime scene?"

She sighed.

"Straight to the point." She gave a little shrug and raised her eyebrows. "I was following the victim."

He frowned and opened the folder.

"Dana Brockers. 22-year-old college student, moonlighting as a dancer at Dougie's Gentlemen's Club."

Tracy sat in silence while he continued reading quietly.

"In your statement, you said you were being paid to keep an eye on her." He stopped reading and looked up at her. "Who were you working for?"

She frowned at him.

"I can't tell you that."

He raised his eyebrows and sat back in his seat.

"How's that?"

She gave him an apologetic shrug.

"They made me sign a non-disclosure agreement."

John shook his head a little.

"I don't give a shit, Tracy. A young woman is dead, and I want to know who did it."

She shook her head.

"I understand completely. But I can't help you any more than I already have. The NDA specifically prohibits me from disclosing the identity of my client, and I may face legal consequences if I decide to disclose that information without the client's consent."

He shook his head at her, his face contorted with mild disgust.

"What the hell happened to you, Tracy? You used to be a cop. And now you sound like a fucking lawyer."

She looked at him cooly.

"I'm still me," she said. "Maybe a little wiser."

They sat in silence for a while, each one assessing the other with hard glares. At last, John softened his face and relaxed in his chair.

"I'm sorry," he said. "It's been a long day."

Tracy remained as before, her face closed as she readied for his next assault.

"Listen," he said. "There may be legal exceptions to the NDA that allow you to disclose the information without the client's consent if the information is necessary to assist in the investigation of a crime. We've got legal counsel here. Let me go check."

She shook her head.

"I don't think so."

John sighed.

"God damn it, Tracy."

She frowned at him and softened her own face.

"Listen," she said. "You're going about this the wrong way. I want to know who killed Dana Brockers just as much as you do. And I can assure you, I am not interested in protecting anyone who might be guilty of something like that. You know me better than that."

He looked at her and drummed his fingers on the table.

"Well, give me a lead, at least. Tell me what you can, outside of the NDA."

She took a deep, thoughtful breath.

"Well, if it were me, I suppose I'd start by getting a look at the security video at Dougie's to see if she had any suspicious encounters with one of the customers."

He glared at her.

"I know how to run an investigation. I'm talking about real shit, Tracy. Something to get us going in the right direction. If you've been following this girl, you must know something. Does she have a boyfriend? Was she being stalked?"

She held out her empty hands.

"Honestly, John, I don't have much to offer."

He shook his head.

"Tracy—"

"No," she said. "I mean it. I'd only been on her tail for four days, and I didn't learn much. Her mother committed suicide when she was very young. She was basically raised by an aunt who lives on the other side of the country now. She has friends, but I haven't talked to them because I've been trying to stay out of sight. I haven't even been inside Dougie's. So, I can't tell you anything that's happened there. I just don't have much to offer right now."

He gave an exasperated sigh.

"But someone has paid you to keep an eye on her," he said. "A jealous boyfriend?"

She frowned.

"John, I'm sorry. I just can't get into it. But you know me. If I come to find that my client was involved in any way, I will let you know. That I promise.

He watched her with a wary eye.

"I don't know, Tracy. You have to understand that withholding information like this makes you a person of interest, whether you're directly involved or not. We'll have to keep an eye on you. That's just the way it is. There's no way around it."

She nodded.

"I know. But just give me some time, ok? Give me some time, and I'll feed you whatever I can. I want to help as much as possible, John. But I can't be effective if I've got a tail while I'm investigating. We should really work together on this as much as possible."

He watched her with that same wary look and then finally let out a slow sigh.

"Fine," he said. "I don't really have any alternative, to be honest. You're not a suspect. At least not at this point. And you're not legally required to tell us anything. But, Tracy, I'm warning you. Things are different here now. The new chief is a real boy scout, and he's also a serious hard-ass. Everything is black and white to him. He won't put up with anything in the gray area. It all has to be by the book now. I can't collaborate with a private investigator. And when he finds out you are a witness to this crime and withholding information, he's going to do whatever he can to make you uncomfortable enough to reveal what you know."

She nodded.

"I appreciate the warning."

He stood and collected the folder.

"I'll send someone in to tie up the details," he said. "Then, you can go."

She gave a nod, and he walked to the door, pausing as he placed his hand on the knob.

"It's good to see you," he said as he turned to look at her.

"Yeah," she said. "You too."

He gave a little nod and left the room. Minutes later, a cop escorted her outside, where the horizon grew pink as the sun began its slow climb into the sky. Tracy stepped out into the lot and started toward her car, pausing when her phone began to buzz inside her jacket pocket. With a yawn, she withdrew the device and sighed at the name. She took a look around and then gave the phone a tap.

"Tracy Sterling."

"Hello, Ms. Sterling," said the voice on the other end of the line.

"Hello, Thomas."

"Are you in a position to talk?"

Tracy stopped at her car and opened the door.

"Sure," she said as she sat down inside.

"Good," he said. "We heard about Ms. Brockers. The senator was very saddened to receive the news. We all were. It's terribly unfortunate."

Tracy frowned at her steering wheel.

"Yes," she said. "It is."

"Can you meet me for a quick conversation?" Thomas asked. "It won't take long."

Tracy yawned and rubbed her tired eyes.

"Sure," she said. "Where?"

There's a nice quiet restaurant named Eddie's on Booker and 19th. Do you know the place?"

Tracy started her car.

"No. But I'll find it."

About a half hour later, she stepped into the restaurant. It was a dimly lit, medium-sized place with tall, wide, almost throne-like wooden booths that offered each table a decent level of privacy from other guests. There were old wooden floors beneath her shoes, and they creaked and whined as she stepped across the threshold. A plump-looking woman greeted her with a smile as she approached the hostess

64

stand. And then, she stepped back when Thomas beckoned for her from a booth in the back of the room.

"Ms. Sterling," he shouted.

The place was otherwise empty except for an old couple sipping soup at one of the other booths, and they didn't seem much interested in his shouting, or Tracy, or each other.

Tracy nodded to the hostess and walked to Thomas's booth.

"Thank you for coming," he said as she sat down across from him. "I understand you've been through a lot. I'm sure you're quite tired and understandably disturbed."

Tracy tried to get comfortable in the stiff wooden booth, which seemed less a seat and more like a torture device.

"Yeah," she said. "It hasn't been fun."

Thomas frowned down at his coffee and nodded.

"Yes," he said. "It's so tragic when anyone dies. But when it's someone so young—"

"Why don't we cut the bullshit?" said Tracy.

Thomas looked up and furrowed his brows.

"I'm sorry?"

"You knew that girl was going to be killed. I want to know how you knew."

He frowned.

"I'm sorry. It's as I said before. I'm not at liberty to say."

"Why not?" asked Tracy.

He looked into her eyes and shook his head slowly.

"I'm not at liberty to tell you that either."

She sat back in the rigid booth and eyed him without speaking. The waitress arrived to take her order but paused and turned back around when she saw the way they looked at each other.

"You think something seems a little off here?" Thomas asked at last.

"I think a lot of things seem a lot off," she said.

He nodded and looked down at his coffee.

"I can see why you feel that way. But I can assure you there's nothing nefarious going on. Save for the murder, of course."

She leaned forward and put her forearms on the table. She looked at him and raised her eyebrows.

"Well, you're hiding something. That much is clear. And that's enough to indicate that you have something nefarious to hide. Is it not?"

He shook his head.

"No. It's really not. Although, I can understand why it seems that way. But I can assure you, this is merely the product of an overprotective security team. It's what happens when you're in politics. It breeds paranoia because you have so many people, so many entities who would love to have even the slightest bit of dirt on the senator, so they can weaponize it and bring him down."

Tracy shook her head.

"I don't care about any of that. You hired me to clear his name, but you're making me work with one hand tied behind my back. If the senator really is innocent of any wrongdoing, tell me what I need to know, so I can help him."

Thomas pursed his lips thoughtfully.

"Look," he said. "The senator is a good man, but he's made his share of mistakes in the past. Just like the rest of us. It's my job, and the job of a lot of other people, to protect his image so he can stay in a position to help his constituents."

Tracy flexed her jaw and stared into his eyes.

"It seems like you're telling me he had an affair with Dana Brockers."

Thomas shook his head.

"I most certainly did not say that."

She put a hand out to her side.

"Then, what? What is so bad that you can't tell me? Give me something to go on. If you really want this to go away, you need to point me in the right direction."

Thomas shrugged.

"I'm sorry. I really wish I could help you. But I'm obligated to Senator Jenkins. You'll have to do this yourself."

Tracy sighed and shook her head.

"Why are you bending over backward for this man?" she asked. "He must pay well."

Thomas frowned down at his coffee.

"It's not about the money."

"Then, what is it?" she asked. "What makes him so special that he can get himself embroiled in something like this and still retain your blind faith?"

"Let me tell you about Senator Jenkins," he said as he looked up at her. "My faith in him isn't some whimsical attraction. It's not the product of blind worship, and it's certainly not about earning a

66

paycheck. It's an allegiance, a very real bond, founded on a deep understanding of the man he is and what he stands for.

"His leadership isn't a flashy billboard. It's a steady candle burning in the dark. He's got empathy and a progressive spirit unlike any other. He's a relentless thinker, and he's got a knack for seeing solutions where others see only problems. That, in my view, is what leadership is all about. It's what sets him apart, and it's why, in the turmoil of our current era, we need him at the helm.

"Consider our reality, Ms. Sterling. Wealth disparity is spiraling out of control. Our climate is turning hostile. Social injustice is rampant. These are not just mere headlines; they're a testament to the systemic failures we're grappling with. Senator Jenkins isn't blind to these; he acknowledges them, but more importantly, he's driven to address them.

"You ask me why this man is so important? Why is he so special? Because he has an unwavering faith in the power of the people, in the idea that united, we can overcome even the greatest of challenges. He isn't afraid to question the status quo, to call out hypocrisy and demand accountability. He's got the intellectual tools to decipher the complexity of our problems, and the creativity to engineer solutions that are not just effective but equitable.

"What really sets him apart is his humanity. He sees beyond the statistics, the political machinations. He sees the people, their hopes, their fears. He treats public service not as a steppingstone to personal power, but as a noble calling.

"That's why I am dedicated to his campaign, to his vision. Because his victory isn't just a personal triumph. It's a victory for the collective, for the world that's yearning for a leader of his caliber."

Tracy sat back in her seat and raised her eyebrows.

"No offense, but you sound obsessed. Like someone taken in by a cult leader. He's just a man like everyone else."

Thomas pursed his lips.

"I understand your perspective. I really do. You might think my faith borders on obsession. But I prefer to think of it as conviction. A firm conviction in a man who can, and I believe, will change the world. That's why he's so important."

Tracy looked at him and drummed her fingers on the table.

"So, correct me if I'm wrong. But it sounds like he's got no intentions of stopping at senator."

Thomas shrugged.

"I do anticipate that Senator Jenkins will become President someday. When? I can't say. We'll throw his hat in the ring when the time is right."

Tracy nodded.

"And that can't happen if he's wrapped up in something this unsavory."

Thomas leaned forward and clasped his hands.

"We need this to go away. The easiest way is for you to find a person of interest, maybe more than one, and point the police in that direction."

Tracy nodded.

"Give me the names of the senator's campaign contributors."

Thomas shrugged.

"You can get those through the Federal Election Commission Database. Senators and other political candidates are required to file regular campaign finance reports with the FEC. These reports contain detailed information about campaign contributions, including the names of individual donors and the amounts they contributed."

Tracy shook her head.

"Not just the official donors," she said. "I'm talking about the ones you don't report."

Thomas glared at her.

"I'm sure I don't know what you mean," he said. "But listen. Before you go poking your nose where you shouldn't, I want to urge you to avoid wasting your time with the senator's financial supporters. That won't do anyone any good. Take my advice and focus on the girl herself. That's the quickest and cleanest way to resolve this."

"What do you mean?" asked Tracy.

He shrugged.

"There has to be someone you can paint a target on. A jealous boyfriend, maybe. Or, hell, look where she worked. The men who visit those places develop fixations on the dancers all the time. A woman like her probably had a couple dozen stalkers."

Tracy shook her head.

"I appreciate the tips," she said flatly. "Now, if you don't mind, it's been a long night. So, if there's not anything else, I'd like to get a little sleep before I dive back into this shit show."

Thomas nodded.

"Yes, of course. I understand."

She stood up and looked down at him.

"Listen," she said. "I can appreciate your position, and I'll definitely look into the possibility of a stalker. But you need to understand that if this leads to one of the senator's supporters, then there's not much I can do about that."

Thomas frowned up at her.

"I understand," he said. "But let me give you some advice if I may."

She shrugged.

"Go ahead."

"I called you because I wanted to talk to you first. But I would expect that you will be hearing from Emmerich soon. As the senator's head of security, he likes to have his fingers in many pies, if you will. He will want to debrief you. He will want an update on things. And when you visit with him, I would not mention your intentions to investigate the senator's campaign donors. It won't go over well."

Tracy yawned.

"Duly noted," she said. "Now, I need to go get some sleep."

Thomas nodded.

"Then, what will you do?" he asked. "It doesn't seem like you have much to go on. I mean that as no offense."

She looked at him.

"Don't worry. I have something in mind."

Chapter 6

Senator Jenkins crossed the large stage and approached the podium, his hands waving as the crowd erupted in raucous applause. This went on for a while, until he finally cleared his throat and leaned closer to the microphone.

"Ladies and gentlemen, fellow citizens and friends."

A hush fell over the mass of humanity as they watched him straighten before the podium. He looked all around and gave a practiced down-home smile, his blue eyes twinkling, hair parted neatly to one side.

"Thank you for joining me here today. It is a true honor to stand before you, not only as your senator but as a fellow American, committed to making our nation a better place for us all. I stand before you with a heart full of hope and determination, for I believe that together, we can create a future that is brighter, fairer, and more prosperous than ever before. We are a nation of dreamers, innovators, and believers – and it is time that we harness that energy and spirit to bring about the change we so desperately need."

The crowd erupted in cheers, signs waving madly, little babies crying, screaming faces painted red, white and blue. The senator raised his hands, and a hush fell over the crowd.

"My fellow Americans, we have reached a critical juncture in our nation's history. We face challenges that have tested our resolve and our unity. But as we look to the horizon, we must remind ourselves that we are a nation of resilience, bound by the shared belief that every person, regardless of their background or circumstances, should have an equal opportunity to thrive.

"We gather here today, united by our common goal: to work for the people, to make positive changes in the lives of our citizens, and to ensure that our democracy remains strong and vibrant. Our nation's strength lies in the hands of ordinary men and women who work tirelessly to create a better future for their families, their communities, and their country.

"As we face the upcoming election, we must recognize the importance of our choices. We stand at a crossroads, where our decisions today will shape the lives of generations to come. My opponent has presented his vision for the future, and now it is time for us to consider the direction we want our nation to take. We must choose between two different paths: one that leads to division and stagnation or one that leads to unity and progress.

"My friends, I stand before you as someone who has dedicated his life to public service, fighting for the common good and the well-being of our communities. I have seen firsthand the power of people coming together to address our most pressing issues. I have witnessed the indomitable spirit of the American people, and I believe that together, we can overcome any obstacle and create a future that is worthy of our highest aspirations.

"As your senator, I have worked to improve the lives of my constituents and the nation as a whole. I have fought for access to quality healthcare, for affordable housing, and for the protection of our environment. I have worked tirelessly to promote education, so that every child has the opportunity to reach their full potential. And I have advocated for policies that create jobs and bolster our economy, ensuring that hardworking Americans can build a better life for themselves and their families.

"But there is still so much work to be done. We must continue to invest in our infrastructure, creating jobs and revitalizing our communities. We must address the growing energy crisis, and take steps to ensure that every able-bodied person has access to respectable jobs that offer fair pay. We must also commit to ensuring that our democracy remains strong and that every voice is heard. We cannot allow the forces of division to tear us apart, for it is only through unity and a common purpose that we can truly achieve greatness. As your

Senator, I will fight every day to ensure that your voice is heard and that your needs are met."

He paused for a moment, and his face turned somewhat somber, his eyes vibrant blue and seeming powerful enough to pierce a person's very soul.

"Now, as we approach this pivotal election, I ask for your support. Together, we can build a better future for our families, our communities, and our nation. We can create a society that is more just, more compassionate, and more prosperous for all.

"Let us stand together, united by our shared values and our common dreams, and let us march forward with hope in our hearts and determination in our steps. Let us commit ourselves to the pursuit of a brighter tomorrow, where opportunity is available to all and where the promise of the American Dream is realized for each and every citizen.

"I humbly ask for your vote, not just as a vote for me, but as a vote for the future we all believe in. This is not about one person or one party; this is about the collective power we hold as a nation to shape our destiny. It's about standing up for what is right, and pushing forward with unwavering determination.

"So, I invite you all to join me on this journey to fight for the America we know we can be. Let us roll up our sleeves, work together, and forge a brighter future for ourselves and generations to come. It will not be easy, and it will not happen overnight, but I have faith in the power of the American spirit and the resilience of our people.

"Together, we will overcome the challenges that lie ahead. Together, we will make our communities stronger, our nation more unified, and our future brighter than ever before. And together, we will prove that the best days of our great country still lie ahead.

"Thank you, God bless you all, and God bless the United States of America."

While the crowd erupted in applause, Tracy stood before the television and watched as the senator shook hands with eager supporters, his brilliant blue eyes glittering as he met each face with what seemed like genuine interest. As people cheered, he continued to move through the crowd, offering out sweaty handshakes and wide, practiced smiles. Someone held up a baby, and he gave it a kiss. A man asked for his autograph, and he happily obliged.

At last, Tracy shook her head and turned off the television, her eyes studying the man's face until the screen winked black. Then, she slipped her pistol into her purse and left her apartment.

It was early evening when she pulled into the parking lot at Dougie's. She sat in her car and waited, while the sun's last fiery tendrils slipped below the horizon. In a matter of moments, dusk enveloped the world in its cooling embrace, draining all the vibrant hues from the sky.

While she sat and watched from the back of the lot, the azure canvas of day quickly faded to black, and celestial diamonds began piercing the deepening twilight. In that ephemeral moment between day and night, she forced herself to breathe as her eyes watched the line of men shuffle past the great bouncer, his tattooed arms folded across his chest like a pair of muscled pythons.

With a sigh, she cracked open her door and stepped out into the night. She clutched her purse against her side to feel the reassuring weight of her gun. Then, she stuffed a wad of chewing gum in her mouth and made her way toward the front of the building.

Heads turned as she approached the line of men, her high heels clacking the pavement, a line of cleavage poking over the top of her low-cut blouse. A scruffy-looking man gave a low whistle as she approached, a wet grin on his face as his eyes explored the curve of her buttocks beneath the thin veneer of her tight denim blue jeans.

The bouncer watched with indifference as she approached, his lower lip pushed out as she cut before the others and stopped at the front of the line.

"Can I help you with something?" he asked in a voice filled with gravel.

"I'm looking for work," said Tracy as she smacked her gum.

The bouncer raised his eyebrows.

"Dancer or server?"

Tracy blew a small pink bubble and shrugged as it popped.

"Whatever."

The bouncer looked her up and down.

"Alright," he said as he stepped aside. 'Ask for Paolo. He does the hiring."

The big man stepped aside, and Tracy moved past, her hips swaying as she disappeared into a fog of cigarette smoke.

Inside, things were less than what she expected. Large and dark, the club was really just a sprawling room with three stages and several small, round, high-top tables. The light was low and mostly coming from the branded neon beer signs that buzzed from the walls behind the long sticky bar. It was the kind of place where you don't know whether it's night or day outside. And the low light turned the guests into featureless silhouettes that wandered about like horny apparitions amid a dense fog of smoke machines and burning tobacco.

She crossed the room, weaving through a crowd of leering men, their heads whipping toward her, as if towed by some exotic gravity. Without acknowledging their glances, she made her way over to the bar and pressed her stomach against the cold rail. With a feminine gesture, she lured the bartender over and ordered a drink. When it came, she downed the entire thing in one big swallow, the alcohol sifting through her vasculature and easing her nerves.

Across the bar, she saw a man in a cheap suit eying her, his jaw square, a runny smile bleeding from the corner of his lips. She shivered as she set her glass down, his lewd gaze traveling her body as he ran his tongue over his bright white teeth. She let her lip curl up before showing him her back. And then, the lights winked out, and the place erupted in noise.

She turned her head with all the rest, as splashes of red light soaked one of the three stages. Out of a billowing white fog, one of the dancers strutted forward, the thumping speakers at pace with her every step.

The stunning girl wore a pair of lacy purple panties and a matching bra, her breasts spilling over the top like great jiggling boulders. The crowd of men gasped as she approached the chrome pole, which jutted from the stage floor like an ill-placed support column. In an instant, she scaled the thing and wrapped her legs around the cold metal, her long blonde hair spilling downward as she leaned back, the line of her cleavage square to the crowd.

As the men beat their hands together, the buxom blonde traveled the pole with a practiced sexuality that promised anything and everything amid a storm of whistles and catcalls.

The beat of the music seemed to crescendo until it felt like a great thumping heart in the room. And then, suddenly, the beat fell silent when a fight broke out in the crowd.

As if someone had flipped a switch, the seductive atmosphere gave way to chaos. Screams pierced the air, and drinks flew as fists pounded bodies, and chairs crashed onto the floor.

The crowd groaned as the dancer wrapped an arm over her breasts and fled the stage. People scrambled to get away from the brawlers but were pushed back toward them by others desperate to get out of harm's way.

Tracy felt a jolt as she was caught up in this chaotic whirlwind, her body washed backward by a wave of men, their faces lit up with glee over the violence unfolding before them.

As she struggled to stay on her feet, Tracy watched the two men throw punches with wild abandon, their eyes wide and filled with rage. Their grappling bodies seemed to become one big flailing entity as they tumbled into a nearby table, glasses shattering into glittering fragments as they crashed to the floor.

Tracy backed away slowly until she felt a wall press against her back. And then, two enormous men approached from opposite directions, their huge hands tossing onlookers aside as they cut through the mob toward the grappling men. With shocking ease, the giants separated the fighters and dragged them outside.

Then, as if they'd witnessed the most ordinary of happenings, everyone turned back to the stage, where another even bustier dancer was strutting out to the beat of a fresh song.

Tracy shook her head and returned to the bar. She ordered another drink, while men bombarded the gyrating dancer with a hail of crumpled one-dollar bills. This went on for several minutes, until the woman was entirely nude, and the stage was carpeted with crumpled cash. When the music died, the dancer collapsed to her knees and clawed the money into a heaping pile. Then, she squeezed her earnings against her bare breasts and left the stage to an explosion of whistles and cheers.

Tracy downed her second drink and looked around, her mind struggling to reconcile that Dana Brockers had been on that very stage just two days before.

She took a deep breath, her eyes squinting into the low light as she surveyed the room. At the far end, one of the dancers was leading a customer toward a narrow hallway aglow with dull red light. All giggles and smiles, the luscious young woman walked with a little bounce as she towed the drooling man forward down the corridor, where they disappeared from sight.

When the speakers began thumping again, Tracy casually made her way toward the narrow red hallway, her fingers trailing over the sticky, wet surface of the bar as she moved to the other side of the club.

While the music roared, a fresh dancer stomped out onto the stage, this one long and muscular and riddled with intricate tattoos.

While her gravity summoned the attention of the room, Tracy pushed away from the bar and moved swiftly toward the red hallway.

The smoke parted as she moved through the crowd, the thick scent of cigars and cigarettes mingling with the musk of colognes, spilled whiskey and the occasional waft of marijuana.

When Tracy reached the hallway, she passed inside as if she'd done so a thousand times, her demeanor casual and relaxed, despite her rapid heart rate. The passage seemed to swallow her up, and she immediately felt claustrophobic. She inhaled deeply and moved forward, her eyes struggling to acclimate to the vibrating red light as she clutched her purse to her side.

There were little rooms on both sides of the hall, each concealed by thick maroon curtains, which obscured the happenings within. Pausing at one of the rooms, Tracy peeled back the edge of the curtain just a touch. Inside, a pair of men clustered around a table, their faces bent low as they snorted lines of cocaine in orderly turns.

Off to the side, another man sat in a chair, while one of the club's dancers straddled his lap, his face buried between her nude breasts, which were heavily dusted with white powder.

Just as one of the men began to raise his head, Tracy released the curtain and backed away. Then, without pausing, she proceeded down the red hallway, her ears picking up the faint sounds of low animal moans amid the deafening boom from the enormous speakers behind her.

As she moved deeper down the hallway, two beautiful young girls emerged from one of the curtained rooms, their hands cupping a pair of giggling mouths. Without acknowledging her, they passed and made their way back out into the main room.

Tracy stopped and watched them disappear around the corner. Then, she turned and pushed onward, her attention gravitating toward a series of low moans coming from behind another pair of curtains.

Carefully, she pulled back the edge and peered around the red fabric. Inside, a bearded man stood pinned against the far wall, while a slim blonde knelt before him, her bare knees naked against the cold concrete floor.

Tracy watched as the man raised his chin and grunted, the girl's head bobbing up and down as her lips worked his manhood. While she bobbed, the man's hands gripped a set of metal water pipes that ran the ceiling overhead.

With each stroke of her mouth, the man tugged the pipes, sending a metallic rattle down the line. His groans turned to whimpers as her hands traveled upward, her fingernails raking against his bare chest, leaving visible lines that were certain to remain for at least a week thereafter.

Tracy watched as the blonde's right hand danced upward on delicate fingers, finally settling on one of the man's nipples. He groaned as she took it between her thumb and finger. As if tuning an old radio, she pinched and twisted, his body wriggling away, trying to escape the pain without success.

Soon his right hand had found its way to the back of her head, but it wasn't pushing; it was pulling her away by the hair.

"Slow down," he begged, but the woman only sped her pace, consuming him nearly whole with every gulp. Within seconds, he was at his end, an easy groan pouring out his open mouth as his body hardened and fell backward against the brick wall.

With what seemed like a practiced giggle, the woman wiped her mouth and stood, surveying the crisscrossed fingernail markings on the man's chest. Then, she leaned in and kissed his lips hard and without apology, his taste still fresh on her thick, red lips.

"What are you doing back here?" asked a hard voice.

Tracy felt her heart leap into her throat as she turned to see a hulking, dark-haired man looking down at her with an accusing stare.

"I was looking for Paolo," she said, a catch in her throat that could not have been missed.

The man's eyes looked like black wells of oil in the dim red light, and he narrowed the flesh around them until he seemed almost demonic. She tried to look into those depthless eyes, her expression one of forced nonchalance as he assessed her with a tilt of the head.

"This is the club's VIP area," he said. "You are not allowed back here."

Tracy smacked her gum and shrugged.

"You should put a sign up."

The man showed his teeth.

"There is a sign."

Tracy shrugged again.

"I must have missed it."

The man watched her without speaking, his jaw covered with stubble, greasy black hair slicked back over his big bulbous skull.

"I'm looking for work," said Tracy. "They said to see Paolo."

77

"I am Paolo," said the man.

Tracy stuck a hand out.

"Megan."

The man looked down at her hand without taking it.

"This way," he said as he turned and walked away.

Tracy dropped her hand and followed him out of the red hallway, the smell of sex drifting away as she pushed back into the noisy main room. They made their way across the club and down another hallway, this one painted black and barely lit by a weak set of overhead bulbs.

Paolo paused before a door and banged his fist against it.

"Vincent," he said.

"Yeah," said a gravelly voice from inside.

Paolo spun the handle and opened the door. He turned sideways and held a hand out. Tracy smacked her gum and strode past him, her eyes looking around the small office before settling on the man behind a big metal desk.

His face was wide and framed by a neatly trimmed beard, which did little to conceal the pale white scar running down the length of one cheek. He wore a tailored gray suit vest over a fine silk maroon dress shirt. But, to Tracy's eyes, he looked like someone better suited to bright orange prison garb.

He resembled a bully she had known in her youth, and his deep brown eyes devoured everything they saw. She forced herself to look into those eyes, which seemed very much like the expressionless pits that killers bore. They were not windows to the soul. Or if they were, there was nothing at the bottom.

"This the one?" Vincent asked without sliding his glare from Tracy.

Paolo nodded.

"Yeah," he said as he shut the door. "Says she's lookin for work."

Vincent nodded and gestured toward a stiff-looking chair on the opposite side of his desk.

"Have a seat."

Tracy sat and placed her purse on her lap. Paolo folded his arms and leaned against the closed door, while Vincent assessed Tracy with the hint of a curly smile.

"Well, I may have something for you," he said. "But I don't think you're really looking for a job, are you?"

Tracy shook her head slowly.

"No."

He smiled, revealing two gold molars set in perfect rows. It was a very unpleasant smile, and Tracy struggled to keep from squirming in her seat.

"And your name is not Megan, either" he said. "It's Tracy."

He made the word 'Tracy' sound like a disease as he spoke it, his eyes leering at her with smug satisfaction.

"That's correct," she said.

He sat back and shrugged.

"So, why are you really here?"

The hard chair was like some rudimentary torture device, and Tracy shifted to keep her ass from going numb. She cleared her throat and raised her eyebrows.

"One of your girls was killed the other night. I'm trying to find out who did it."

He shrugged.

"I am aware of this," he said. "And I'm not happy about it. It's bad for business, after all. We will find the person responsible. I can assure you of that. And I will deal with him personally. It's my business now. You needn't concern yourself with it."

Tracy shrugged.

"Nonetheless, I have a job to do."

Vincent sneered at her. He had a very effective sneer.

"And what is it you expect from me?"

She raised her eyebrows.

"I want to look at your security footage."

The cruel-looking man gave a laugh that would have chilled the devil, his face showing sincere amusement.

"Is that all?" he asked. "You don't want to take a look at my accounting as well?"

Tracy shrugged.

"If there's time, why not?"

His face soured, and he sat up in his chair.

"Why would I want to help you?"

Tracy raised her eyebrows.

"I have money," she said. "Let me make it worth your while."

He chuckled.

"Do you know how much I make in a single night? Not just at this place, either. I own three different clubs throughout the city."

She shrugged.

"All right, then," she said. "I witnessed at least three different crimes just walking across the floor of this place. Show me the security footage, and I'll keep it to myself."

Vincent leaned closer and let his eyes bore into hers. He watched her for a moment and breathed, the deep silence deafening in her ears. Then, at last, he gave another chilling smile and folded his hands on the desk.

"Let me give you some advice," he said. "Or maybe it's perspective. Is it perspective? I don't know. Either way, you should hear it."

He took in a deep breath without breaking eye contact.

"Sometimes," he said, "people make mistakes about where they are powerful and where they are weak. I myself have made this error from time to time. And these errors brought lessons that were hard and lasting."

He raised a finger to where the pale scar split his face.

"Now," he continued, "you may have felt powerful at times in your life. When you handcuffed a man, perhaps. When you killed that boy from the news. But here, Ms. Sterling, you are not powerful. Here, in this place, you are to me like an insect between my fingers."

He looked past her to Paolo, who immediately turned and locked the door. Tracy's hand drifted toward her purse, but Vincent didn't seem to notice. Or if he did, his face showed no concern. Instead, he pushed back in his chair and rubbed his head, as if weary from the conversation. He gave a great sigh as his eyes drifted toward the ceiling.

"The cops in this city are like a plague of locusts," he said. "They descend from time to time to devour all I have grown. And for this reason, I do not allow any security cameras in my place. It is incriminating, and it makes the customers uncomfortable. It also gives the police something to use against us in the court of law. Or to extort us for money under the table."

His eyes fell upon her like a hammer.

"You and your like have extorted me for years," he said. "And now you come to me for favors?"

Tracy opened her mouth to speak, but stopped when she felt one of Paolo's large hands envelop her shoulder from behind. Vincent sat back in his chair and looked over her body, his eyes seeming to assess the slope of her breasts beneath her blouse as he tilted his head to the side.

"I'm a curious guy," he said. "I wonder about certain things sometimes. Things I think sane men should not wonder about. But alas, I wonder about them just the same."

Tracy's hand trickled inside her purse, and the tips grazed the pistol within. As if privy to her very thoughts, Paolo responded with a painful squeeze, only ceasing when she froze. Vincent continued to look at Tracy's chest, his eyes narrowing as he pushed his bottom lip out.

"Right now," he said. "I am wondering if it feels the same to kill an ex-cop as it does an actual cop? If the knife slides in any faster. If the blood would spurt like a fountain or seep out like a clogged drain. I know the repercussions would be different. But the feeling? Would there be a rush? Or would it feel like any other ordinary person? That would be disappointing."

The room fell quiet for a long time. Long enough for Tracy to go mad from the sound of her heart pounding in her ears. Long enough for sweat to gather and dribble down her forehead.

At last, Vincent raised his upper lip and showed his teeth.

"Go," he said. "Leave here while you still can."

Without another word, Tracy stood and turned toward the door. Paolo watched her with a little smirk as she moved past and slipped like smoke through the door.

Outside the office, she pushed through the crowd of drunken men on her way to the club entrance, while anonymous hands pawed at her backside. When she finally popped out into the night, the bouncer regarded her without much interest as she hurried away from the entrance and out into the parking lot.

She reached her car and climbed inside, locking the door as she settled in her seat. She sat for a moment and breathed, the smell of cigarette smoke emanating from her hair and filling the interior with a noxious stink. Her breathing quickened as she felt the gorge rising in her stomach. Almost too late, she opened the door and emptied her stomach onto the blacktop. Then, she started the engine and made the long drive home.

Chapter 7

Tracy sat in her car listening to the rain. It was late afternoon, and the long-threatening skies had finally opened up, bathing the city in a cold, drenching downpour. High away, the heavens were closed by a shaggy blanket of gray clouds, and the dim streetlights had already popped on in response to the premature evening.

She gazed out through the bleary windshield and watched as people hurried across the parking lot and into the little gas station. Some had umbrellas, while others held briefcases over their heads.

She yawned at them and rubbed her eyes. The night had been long, and her sleep had been plagued by ugly dreams. Vincent's harsh face split by a cruel grin. Dana's cut throat gushing blood as her bright red hair faded to a dull gray.

She swallowed and rubbed her eyes, stopping when she heard the tap at the window. In an automated way, her hand moved to her pistol, as she flinched away from the passenger window. There stood Jimmy, his big body sheathed in a long dark coat that looked old and weathered and slick with rain.

Tracy unlocked the car, and he yanked the door open. she watched as he climbed inside with a grunt, the fog of his breath gathering on the windshield as he shut himself inside. He coughed and shook off some of the rain as he looked at her.

"What's wrong with your apartment?" he asked. "Or a diner, for Christ's sake?"

Tracy shook her head.

"I don't want to be seen with you."

Jimmy raised his eyebrows.

"Thanks."

She frowned.

"It's not like that. It's this case I'm working on. It's got me a little paranoid."

He watched her.

"And desperate too, apparently," he said. "I mean, you must be desperate if you're working with that Tony piece of shit."

Tracy sighed.

"I was in a spot. I didn't have time to be choosy."

He nodded.

"Alright," he said. "Why am I here? Same reason?"

She shrugged.

"Maybe."

Jimmy turned his head toward the window. Outside, the puddles glittered beneath the light as they gathered rain.

"Well," he said. "Lay it on me, I guess. Unless you want to talk about the weather."

Tracy took a deep breath and told him all about the case. About Vincent and his threats. The senator and his people. Dana Brockers and her gashed throat. When she was finished, he sat for a long time thinking while the rain thrummed down from overhead, his face closed and expressionless in a way that made her curiously angry.

"Well?" she asked.

He shrugged.

"Well, what?"

She gave an exasperated sigh.

"This is a shit show," she said. "I'd value your input."

"Of course, it's a shit show," said Jimmy. "That's why I passed on it."

She turned toward him.

"You were offered the job?"

He shrugged.

"I was invited to the senator's mansion. I left as soon as I realized I wasn't the only one."

Tracy shook her head.

"You must have left just before I got there."

Jimmy scratched his jaw.

"Yeah, well, I'm not much for tests."

Outside, rain lashed the city streets, filling the gutters with a brown slurry of cigarette butts, discarded wrappers and rotting leaves. Within those gutters, the rivers of sludge bubbled and whirled their way down into the slurping drains and into the city's bowels.

Tracy sighed.

"Ok," she said. "What's it gonna take to get your input?"

He thought for a moment.

"Three-hundred dollars for now," he said. "If it goes past tonight, we'll revisit the terms."

She frowned at him.

"You're quite a friend, Jimmy."

He shrugged.

"A man's gotta eat."

She nodded.

"Ok. Done."

She passed over the money, and he counted it before slipping it into his coat pocket.

"Alright," he said. "What do you want from me?"

She raised her eyebrows.

"Why don't you start by telling me who you think might have killed Dana Brockers?"

He scratched his jaw.

"Why don't you tell me what you think first?"

Tracy sat back in her seat and looked at him.

"Alright," she said. "The most obvious conclusion is the senator hired someone to kill Dana because he was having an affair with her, and she threatened to go public."

Jimmy nodded.

"But why would he hire you beforehand? He essentially made himself a suspect by choosing to do that. It doesn't make a whole lot of sense."

Tracy shook her head.

"It doesn't matter," she said. "I've looked into this girl's life. There are no jealous boyfriends. There are no enemies that would want her dead. My first thought in a case like this would be that one of the club's regulars developed a fixation on her that turned violent. But how would that explain the senator's suspicions that she was in danger? The fact that his staff warned me about her impending murder has

84

essentially cleared any other potential suspect and implicated the senator himself."

Jimmy frowned.

"But for the sake of argument," he said, "let's assume your senator really is innocent."

Tracy turned a hand over.

"If Senator Jenkins didn't kill this woman or at least have some hand in it, then who did?"

Jimmy shrugged.

"Someone looking out for his interests. Or protecting their own."

"How do you mean?" asked Tracy.

Jimmy looked at her and furrowed his brows.

"Tracy, come on. There are a lot of special interests tied to a senator. Companies. Organized criminals. Anyone who stands to profit from his continued success or suffer from his failures. Maybe they want him to stay in power because it benefits them. Maybe they want something to hold over his head as leverage to control him to some degree."

Tracy frowned thoughtfully.

"So, I look at his supporters? That's a pretty big pool of suspects."

Jimmy nodded.

"Oh yeah," he said. "It could be almost anyone. A pharmaceutical company that wants him to help get their drug approved. A land developer that wants to build on a nature reserve. A bank that wants less regulation. An oil company that wants to drill. A chemical company that wants to dump. The possibilities are endless. That's why this case is a loser that you should have declined right at the outset."

Tracy sighed and sat back in her seat, while raindrops popped against the roof of the car.

"What a mess."

Jimmy nodded.

"Yep," he said. "And even if you did have a lead, you'd be taking an enormous risk by pursuing it."

She raised her eyebrows.

"There's always risk."

He shook his head.

"Not like this. These are deep waters you're planning to swim in. This client, in particular, will have a lot of powerful enemies. Way too powerful for you to go poking around into their business."

"Be specific," she said. "What enemies?"

Jimmy shrugged.

"Political rivals. Corporations that don't like his policies. Plenty of people who'd like to destroy him by having this girl killed and pinning it on him."

"Corporations have people killed?" asked Tracy. "Are you a conspiracy theorist now?"

Jimmy chuckled.

"Don't be naive."

Tracy rubbed her eyes and shook her head as she thought about all the digging she'd already done. The senator did indeed have many supporters with deep pockets, and she had spent the better part of an afternoon looking into several of them. There was Vioxx Genomics, a major pharmaceutical and genetic research company. There was an organization known as NPG, which didn't seem to do much at all except donate to major political campaigns. There were corporations, wealthy individuals and unions, all of which had donated huge sums of money to the senator or his rivals. And there were countless other entities that might be actual companies, or perhaps fake companies that were really just political action committees formed to raise and spend money to influence elections.

"This keeps getting worse and worse," she said.

Jimmy raised his eyebrows.

"I'm just getting started," he said. "This senator could also have ties to organized crime."

She looked at him.

"Wouldn't you get wind of something like that? I mean, considering your connections."

He shrugged.

"I don't have any inside information. I'm just saying it's always a possibility. Organized criminals are really just corporations. They want regulators to look the other way. And they want policies that promote their businesses and protect their little cartels. All these businesses have interests, and they guard them however they can, whether it's drugs, oil or chocolate candy bars."

Tracy frowned at this.

"So, one of the senator's enemies catches him in an affair with Dana Brockers and then decides to kill her to frame him? Seems like a reach."

Jimmy shrugged.

"They may have arranged the affair. The girl was probably on their payroll."

She shook her head.

"Always so positive. You haven't changed a bit."

He shrugged again and looked out at the rain.

"Okay," said Tracy, "Let's say a political enemy paid this girl to fuck him. Why kill her? Why not just publicize the affair?"

Jimmy shrugged.

"Politics is complicated these days. An affair may not be enough to torpedo a campaign."

"But a murder would," said Tracy.

Jimmy nodded.

"One can only hope."

Tracy sat back in her chair and gave an exasperated sigh.

"Jesus Christ," she said. "This is a fucking conspiracy."

Jimmy frowned.

"Maybe," he said. "Or maybe the senator really did have her killed."

Tracy looked at him.

"Then why hire me?"

"Who knows?" said Jimmy. "To make it look like he's innocent? To have someone on his side in the courtroom? You said yourself, his lawyer observed your testimony the day he approached you."

Tracy shook her head.

"So, you've basically given me an endless lineup of potential suspects and told me they're all too powerful to investigate, and there's no way to solve this case."

He frowned.

"I told you this case was a dumper."

Tracy looked out the window and frowned.

"If only Dougie's had security footage. There might have been a lead there."

Jimmy furrowed his brow.

"Oh, they have footage."

Tracy looked over at him.

"What are you talking about?" she asked. "Vincent said they didn't."

Jimmy just looked at her with his dead man's eyes.

"Did he?"

They sat for a while without talking while the rain pummelled the streets. Lightning crackled in the sky, and people flinched as they hurried across the parking lot. Tracy eyed Jimmy while the heavens rumbled overhead.

"How can I get that footage?" she asked.

Jimmy frowned thoughtfully.

"I can get it," he said.

"How?" asked Tracy.

He raised his eyebrows.

"First, let's talk money."

Tracy sighed.

"Why don't you just come in on this case with me?" she asked. "We'll work together, and I'll give you 50 percent of everything."

Jimmy shook his head.

"I didn't want this case when it was 100 percent of everything."

Tracy rubbed her head.

"Ok, then," she said. "How do you want to do this?"

He shrugged.

"It's your case, but I'm willing to help here and there in a piecemeal sort of way. You pay me as we go. But if I'm being honest, I don't think this case gets solved. So, I don't want to be associated with it. No offense. That's just how I feel about things."

Tracy nodded.

"Fair enough," she said. "How much will it cost to get the security footage from Dougie's? If it really exists like you say."

Jimmy scratched his bald head.

"Oh," he said. "That'd probably run you two grand."

Tracy sighed.

"Two thousand dollars?" she asked. "That's kind of steep, isn't it?"

He frowned at her.

"Maybe. But what choice have you got?"

She sat back in her seat and shook her head.

"Fine," she said. "But how in the hell are you going to get it?"

He shrugged.

"I'm gonna ask him for it."

She looked at him as if he'd just grown a second head.

"Ask him for it? Just like that?"

"Just like that," he said as he looked at her with his dead, expressionless eyes. "And you're coming with me."

Chapter 8

They arrived at Dougie's near closing time. It was very late, but there were still plenty of vehicles in the lot, and their hoods glinted beneath a pale crescent moon, which hung high away in the clear, quiet sky. Tracy brought the car to a halt and looked around. The lighting was poor, and the dark stretch of blacktop unfolded like some sinister setting for dark events. She took a deep breath and looked over at Jimmy, who yawned and scratched his jaw.

"You sure about this?" she asked.

He looked at her with his usual expressionless face.

"Relax," he said. "Just let me do the talking."

They stepped out of the vehicle and made their way to the front of the club, where the same big bouncer stood with his arms folded. There was no line outside the club, and he looked half asleep as he leaned back against the building. But he straightened at the sound of their footsteps, and Tracy felt her heart pick up as he pushed away from the building.

The big man seemed to swell in size as he saw them approach, his eyes narrowing as they emerged from the night. He took a few steps forward and paused to block their path.

"The fuck are you doing here?" he asked.

Jimmy stopped and looked up at the man.

"I'm here to talk to your boss," he said.

The man's muscles flexed beneath his shirt like writhing snakes, and he flashed his teeth at Jimmy, who rewarded the threatening gesture with his boredest expression yet.

"You're not going in there," said the bouncer. "Not after the trouble you caus—"

The man's face turned bright red as Jimmy's knee drove upward into his groin. Tracy watched in silence as the bouncer collapsed to his knees and wheezed for breath.

Jimmy frowned down at him and then turned toward Tracy. "Let's go."

As she followed him toward the entrance. Tracy stole a glance at the enormous man, who had begun to release childish whimpers as he slowly sank lower to the ground. Then, she was through the door and inside the club, where a low haze of cigarette smoke stung her nose and stabbed at her raw, sleep-starved eyes.

Without pausing, Jimmy navigated through the throng of drunken men, Tracy keeping pace as the booming music thumped within her chest. They approached the bar, and Jimmy scanned the room. Most of the men had gathered near the stages, where the girls worked the poles with admirable dexterity amid a hail of crumpled dollar bills.

"Whiskey, neat," Jimmy told the bartender, his voice barely audible over the din. "And something fruity for my friend here."

Tracy glared at him and shook her head.

"I'm fine, thanks."

The bartender nodded and walked away.

"What are we doing?" Tracy asked, her shouting voice struggling to compete with the hammering base of the music.

"Just relax," said Jimmy.

She opened her mouth to say more, but the bartender arrived with Jimmy's drink.

"Paolo here?" he asked.

The bartender, a fat man with a brambly beard, squinted and leaned closer.

"Huh?"

"Paolo here?" Jimmy shouted.

The man pulled away and regarded Jimmy with an uncertain look.

"Who's asking?"

Jimmy ignored the man and took a sweeping look around the club.

"Tell him it's Jimmy."

The bartender frowned and stepped away, while Jimmy lifted his whiskey and drank it down in one big swallow. Tracy watched as the bartender moved to the other side of the bar and whispered into the ear of a scantily clad waitress. Then, the girl disappeared through the crowd, like a little mouse moving through a maze.

"What is the plan here?" asked Tracy.

Jimmy continued looking around the club.

"What plan?"

Tracy raised her eyebrows.

"You don't have a plan?"

Jimmy shrugged.

"Not really."

Tracy looked away and saw Paolo approaching from the far side of the club.

"Shit," she whispered, but her words were lost to the noise.

She made an inconspicuous gesture toward the other side of the club, and Jimmy followed her finger to Paolo, who was pushing drunks aside as he stormed across the floor.

"Just relax," Jimmy said as he pushed away from the bar.

Paolo's eyes bounced from Jimmy to Tracy as he approached, and Tracy could plainly see the gun within his open sport coat.

"Shit," she whispered again.

At last, Paolo settled before them and frowned, his dark, stubbly jaw square and set, the strobing lights from the stage reflecting off his dark, slicked-back hair.

"What are you doing here, Jimmy?" he asked with iron in his hard, raspy voice. "And why is she with you?"

Jimmy squared before him, and they met at the eye.

"I need to see Vincent," Jimmy yelled over the noise.

Paolo shook his head.

"We're all paid up. So, there's nothing for you to discuss."

Jimmy shook his head without taking his eyes from Paolo's.

"This ain't about that."

Paolo glanced over at Tracy and flexed his jaw.

"Then, what's it about?" he asked. "You tell me, and I'll decide if it's worth the boss's time."

Jimmy shook his head.

"Nah," he said. "I'll do it myself."

Tracy watched as the two men stared at each other, their faces painted with intermittent shadows and lights, the bone structures seeming to change shape with each strobing pulse.

"Stay here a second," said Paolo.

He turned and disappeared into the crowd of men, their faces fixated on the stage, hands cupped over their mouths as they yelled and hooted over the deep and deafening thump of the speakers. Tracy watched Paolo leave and then turned to Jimmy.

"What's he talking about?"

Jimmy looked down at her.

"Huh?"

She took hold of his arm.

"He said they're all paid up. What does that mean?"

Jimmy looked into her eyes, his face gargoylian amid the flickers of shadow and lights.

"Later," he said.

She pulled away and watched him, but he had already turned his attention to Paolo, who was forcing his way back through the mob.

"This way," he yelled as he squirted out of the human congestion.

He turned and forced his way back through the throng, Jimmy following, Tracy trailing a few steps behind.

As she moved through the mass of arms and legs, Tracy could smell the tangled scent of drunken breath, cigarette smoke, cheap cologne and sour body odor. And more than a few of the drunken men seized the chance to graze her backside amid the anonymity of the crowd.

At last, they popped out the other side, and Paolo led them down the dimly lit black hallway that led to Vincent's office. When he reached the man's door, he gave it a hard knock, and Tracy felt her heart jump as his fist rang against the wood.

"Yeah," said that gravelly voice from inside.

Paolo turned the handle and opened the door. He turned sideways and held a hand out. Jimmy stepped in first, and Tracy hesitated for a moment before following behind him. Her heart raced as she set eyes on Vincent, who ignored them both as he stared down at a stack of papers. As they stood before his desk, Paolo shut the door and loomed in the space behind them.

A few moments passed, and then Vincent looked up, his soulless eyes glittering as he regarded them both with a friendly smile that looked strangely disturbing on his scarred face.

"Ah, the devil himself," he said, as he looked at Jimmy. "And you brought a friend, I see." His eyes lingered on Tracy, and she struggled not to shudder. "To what do I owe the pleasure? I believe, and correct me if I'm wrong, I'm all paid up this month."

Tracy's eyes flicked from Vincent to Jimmy, but he continued to stare across the desk.

"This ain't about that," Jimmy said.

"No?" asked Vincent. "Then what is it about? Something to do with your friend here? Have you come on her behalf?"

Jimmy shrugged.

"One of your girls got clipped the other night in the parking lot." He gestured toward Tracy. "She's trying to find out why. I'm helping."

Vincent raised his eyebrows and smiled.

"How nice," he said. "I didn't realize you were so compassionate, Jimmy. But as I told Ms. Sterling the other night, that is my business, and I will handle it my way."

Jimmy looked at him with his usual expressionless face.

"I don't care what you do," he said. "But we need to take a look at your security footage from the night she was killed. And a few other nights just to be safe."

Vincent's face darkened, and Paolo folded his arms.

"As I told your friend the other night, we don't keep security cameras. It makes the customers antsy."

Jimmy frowned.

"Oh, I'll bet you can come up with something. If you look hard enough."

Vincent narrowed his eyes.

"And why would I do that?"

Jimmy took a step forward, and Paolo bridled. Vincent raised a hand to gesture him back as Jimmy settled before his desk.

"You owe me, Vincent. This will square things."

Vincent raised his eyebrows.

"Really?" he asked. "You would wipe away this debt for something so trivial?"

Jimmy shrugged, his blank expression betraying nothing.

"Oh, I'm sure something else will come up," he said. "Someone in your line of work always needs a favor eventually."

Vincent glared at him for a moment. Then, his eyes flicked over to Tracy.

"You two are partners now?" he said with a slight chuckle. "A couple of ex-cops. Two peas in a pod."

He narrowed at Tracy, and she struggled to stare into them.

"You think you know this man?" he asked. "You think he is a private investigator? Maybe he is. How many lives live inside a single man, after all? But he is also more than this. Do you know that? No? Let me enlighten you. Despite what he may have told you, he is not a good man. He is not a friend to you or anyone else. He is a fixer. He is a bagman. And he works for people much worse than me."

Tracy shrugged.

"I appreciate your concern," she said. "But I'm not marrying him. We just need the security footage so we can find the person who killed one of your girls."

Vincent sat back in his chair.

"Ok," he said. "Maybe we do have some cameras. And maybe I do have some video somewhere. But if so, I can assure you, my people would have already looked at this hypothetical footage. And there is nothing in them. Just an ordinary night, save for the end. You will be disappointed."

Jimmy shrugged.

"Well, we'll take them off your hands anyway."

Vincent frowned, his eyes bouncing from one to the other as he scratched his bristly jaw.

"Ok," he said.

Paolo straightened.

"Boss, you don't have to give them anything. Let me throw this piece of shit out."

"Shut up," said Vincent.

Jimmy continued staring forward, his face relaxed and unconcerned.

"What do I care?" said Vincent. "You take the footage. There's nothing to see. But if you want to wipe away a debt over something like this, who am I to stand in the way?"

He flicked a hand at Paolo.

"Get the security footage," he said. "No backtalk. It's what I want."

95

Paolo flexed his jaw and nodded. Then, he turned and left the office.

They waited in silence for several minutes, the two big men staring at each other intently as if locked in an absurd contest or some mysterious conversation of the eye. Tracy fidgeted amid the charged air and nearly flinched when Vincent's phone buzzed. Without taking his eyes off Jimmy, he plucked up the receiver and put it to his ear.

"Yeah," he said.

He listened and then hung up the phone.

"Paolo has what you need," he said. "He's waiting outside."

Without a word, Jimmy turned toward the door, Tracy following closely while her heart pounded within her chest.

"Jimmy," said Vincent.

The two paused at the door and turned to see Vincent's grinning face.

"Be careful out there. The world's a dangerous place, even for someone like you."

Without responding, Jimmy turned away and opened the door. Outside the office, Paolo stood with a small USB flash drive. Jimmy looked down at his hand as Tracy shut the door behind them.

"That it?" he asked

Paolo shoved the device into Jimmy's hand.

"Yeah."

Jimmy slipped the flash drive into his coat pocket and looked at Paolo, who watched him with unconcealed hate.

"You got something to say?" asked Jimmy.

Paolo raised his upper lip to show his gleaming white teeth.

"Another time."

Jimmy shrugged.

"Well," he said. "I'm available anytime. Just let me know."

With that, he pushed past Paolo and forced his way through the crowd, Tracy following in his wake as they made their way out of the club.

Outside, the parking lot glowed beneath the pale moon, the vehicles glinting as they walked away from the club. Somewhere amid the cars, an unseen drunk emptied his stomach onto the asphalt. Tracy felt her lip curl as she followed Jimmy, who moved across the lot with an easy manner, as if he'd just had a cordial lunch with a dear old friend.

When they reached Tracy's car, they both got inside and sat for a moment. Tracy held the keys in her hands and breathed as her heart rate finally began to slow.

"Listen," said Jimmy. "About what he said in there—"

Tracy raised a hand.

"Forget it," she said. "I don't care about your business, Jimmy. You want to be a fixer or a bagman for organized criminals, be my guest. I don't need you to explain anything to me. I just need to find this girl's killer."

Jimmy turned away and looked out the window.

"Fair enough," he said.

She took a deep breath and looked over at him.

"Thanks for your help. You definitely earned your money."

He nodded.

"Anytime."

She turned the ignition, and the engine growled to life.

"Where should I drop you?" she asked.

He looked at her and scratched his jaw.

"How bout I stick around a little longer?"

She raised her eyebrows.

"I thought you didn't want in on this case."

He shrugged.

"I don't. But I am a little curious, if I'm being honest. I wouldn't mind seeing how this plays out. Anyway, the way you're approaching things, you may need someone watching your back. Unless you have reservations about me based on tonight."

She shook her head.

"No," she said. "No reservations. I'll take whatever help I can get."

He nodded.

"Well, then, let's go get a look at that footage."

She looked at the clock.

"Now? It's 3 a.m."

He shrugged.

"Sleep is for the weak," he said. "You better learn that if you want to stick as a PI. Anyway, the best breaks in a case always happen after midnight."

"Is that a fact?" she asked as she put the car in reverse.

He looked out the windshield where the parking lot was beginning to thin.

"No," he said. "But it helps to bullshit yourself. It's good for morale."

Chapter 9

It was 4 a.m. when they arrived at Tracy's apartment, and the city still labored amid the lightless pre-dawn. In the near distance, police sirens bloomed up intermittently, flaring in the distance like some ominous white noise that would have been disturbing only in their absence.

With a great yawn, Tracy unlocked the door and tossed her keys onto a table. Without pausing, she rushed across the living room and collected her laptop. She hurried to the kitchen and set it on the table, while Jimmy removed the USB drive and took a seat.

Tracy stood and looked at him with her hands on her hips.

"For someone who doesn't want to be a part of this case, you're sure settling in fast."

He looked up at her.

"I've gone through a thousand of these security videos," he said. "Trust me. It'll be faster if you let me take the lead."

She watched him with a doubtful expression.

"It will take a while to go through a full week of video," she said.

Jimmy nodded as he slipped the drive into the laptop.

"I'll accelerate the video playback. We'll run through it once at high speed in case something obvious jumps out. After that, I'll go through it again real slow and check everything with a fine-toothed comb."

Tracy nodded.

"Fine. Start with the night of her murder. I'll make some coffee."

She went into the kitchen and opened a cabinet. The sparse inventory echoed Tracy's preference for simplicity, although it also whispered a gentle reminder that a trip to the store might soon be unavoidable. A single can of beans sat alongside a half-empty bag of rice, the duo holding their ground as the last remnants of sustenance. It was a sad testament to her minimalist approach to stocking groceries – just enough to keep you from gnawing on your own arm in a fit of hunger.

She sighed and snatched up the box of coffee.

"Cream or sugar?" she asked.

"Black," said Jimmy.

"Of course," Tracy whispered to herself.

She got the machine started and stepped back as it began to whir, a yawn stretching her mouth while she rubbed her tired eyes. As if sensing her fatigue, Jimmy looked over at her.

"Why don't you get some sleep? I can do the first shift."

She looked at him.

"You're not tired?"

He shook his head.

"I don't sleep much. And when I do, it's usually during the day."

She nodded.

"Maybe I will," she said as she approached with his coffee. "You won't steal anything, will you?

He looked around at all the sparsity.

"I'll try to resist."

She nodded and yawned again, just as her phone buzzed.

"Shit," she said.

She picked up the phone and looked at the screen, her brows furrowing as she tried to place the number. Jimmy turned his attention back to the laptop as she put the phone to her ear.

"Tracy Sterling," she said.

"Hello, Ms. Sterling," said a low, quiet voice.

"Hello, Emmerich," she said. "What can I do for you?"

"You can meet me at the diner on 14th and Briar," he said. "Ten minutes."

Tracy sighed.

"Can we do this later? I've been up all night."

"Yes," said Emmerich. "I am aware. But, no. I need to speak to you immediately."

Tracy glanced at Jimmy, who was squinting at the security footage.

"Alright," she said. "14th and Briar."

"That is correct."

"I'll be there shortly," she said as she hung up the phone.

Jimmy looked up at her.

"Who was that?"

She frowned down at him.

"Are we partners now?"

He shook his head.

"Nope."

"Alright, then," she said. "But if you really want to know, it's just the senator's head of security. He probably wants an update on my progress. It won't take too long."

Jimmy nodded.

"I'll keep at it, then."

She left him hunched over the table, his eyes squinting as he scrutinized the security footage.

It was about 20 minutes later when she pulled into the diner at 14th and Briar. Stars still twinkled in the dark morning sky as the faint hint of dawn colored the horizon. She slotted her car in the small parking lot and stared forward, where she could see the strange man, sitting alone at a booth positioned directly before a large window. He wore a black fedora and a long matching trench coat that seemed better suited for a chilly autumn evening than what the rising sun intended for this spring day.

She killed the engine and watched him for a moment, his sharp, bony face seeming especially gaunt from the side as he blew into a hot cup of tea. Tracy rubbed her eyes and stepped outside, where the birds chirped their celebrations as the city began stirring amid the promise of another long day.

A bell above the door tinkled as she stepped into the diner. She paused for a moment and surveyed the setting with her dry, bloodshot eyes. Alone at the breakfast bar, a uniformed delivery man sipped coffee as he read a newspaper. A few feet away, a plump, middle-aged woman fried bacon, her hand stifling some yawns of her own as she worked. Other than that, the place was empty, save for Emmerich, who was watching her with his disturbingly vivid eyes.

Tracy sighed and approached the table.

"Well," she said as she sat down on the opposite side. "I'm here."

He raised the tea to his lips without taking his eyes from her face.

"Yes," he said. "It is good to see that you are capable of arriving on time."

He had a dry, hiss of a voice that was almost too quiet, and Tracy had to lean forward to make out what he was saying.

"What does that mean?" she asked.

He set the tea down and frowned.

"Where were you the other night?" he asked. "When Ms. Brockers was killed? It seems to me you are being paid to surveil her. Yet, when you were needed most, you were absent."

He blew on his tea and then took a slow, delicate sip as if he were sampling scalding broth fresh from the boil.

"I ran into a complication," said Tracy.

He set the cup down and looked into it, his skull of a face wrinkling up in thought.

"A complication," he repeated.

She nodded.

"Yes."

He looked at her.

"How unfortunate. The timing, I mean. Your complication occurred at just the right moment, it seems. Or the wrong one, depending on how you look at it."

Tracy sat back in her seat and watched him.

"Are you saying someone was following me and waiting for an opportunity?"

Emmerich smiled.

"Who would do such a thing?" he said.

Tracy shrugged.

"No one who values their balls."

They watched each other for a few moments. The bell at the door announced the arrival of more customers. Raw bacon crackled and popped on the skillet.

At last, Emmerich spoke.

"Do you not find it strange that you followed Ms. Brockers for four days without incident, only to have her fall victim during the brief interlude of your," he paused for a moment, "complication."

She furrowed her brows.

"Maybe. Maybe not. She was killed leaving work. That could be a coincidence. Unless you know something you're not telling me. Do you know something?"

He stirred his tea and shook his head.

"I know many things," he said. "But I am not here to educate you. I am here to warn you."

Tracy watched as he sipped his tea.

"That I'm being followed?"

His eyes flicked up from his tea. He swallowed and set the cup down.

"No," he said. "But you should be wary of that too."

He took a deep breath.

"No," he continued. "I am here to warn you about your recklessness."

"Recklessness?" she asked.

He frowned at her.

"Shortly after Ms. Brockers was killed, you began looking into supporters of Senator Jenkins."

She nodded.

"Yes."

He raised his eyebrows.

"Why?"

Tracy looked at him.

"You know why."

He continued staring into her eyes, a twinkle of impatience somewhere within.

"Humor me," he said.

Tracy shrugged.

"I was told the senator was innocent and asked to point the police in the right direction," she said. "There are a lot of special interests that profit from the senator's position and others that would like to see him replaced. I'm merely trying to determine if any of these might have cause to either frame him or eliminate someone who might stand in the way of his re-election."

She raised her eyebrows.

"Is that clear enough for you?"

He shook his head slowly, and he straightened before her.

"Ms. Sterling, are you familiar with the concept of private intelligence agencies?"

She nodded.

"I've heard of them, yes."

He studied her with a skeptical eye and then took in a long, slow breath.

"You've heard of them," he said dryly. "That's nice. But I will now ask you to humor me a little more as I attempt to enlighten you further."

She casually flipped her hand over as if to give permission. He flexed his jaw in frustration, and there was no hiding the gesture beneath his thin, pale flesh.

"You may or may not know," he began, "that a private intelligence agency, as the name implies, is a privately-owned company that provides intelligence and investigative services to clients such as corporations, law firms, government agencies and very wealthy individuals. These agencies purport to conduct research, analysis, surveillance, and other types of intelligence-gathering activities to provide their clients with information that can help them make informed decisions or take specific actions."

He glared at her.

"This is what they purport to do."

Tracy eyed him.

"But they also kill people," she said. "Is that what you're driving at?"

He shrugged.

"These agencies can be involved in a range of activities such as corporate espionage, competitive intelligence, due diligence investigations, fraud detection and risk assessment. They are often used to gather information, including public records, human intelligence, and technical surveillance. But whatever the case, they are not government-owned and operated organizations, although they often employ former agents from the military and CIA."

Tracy watched him, but much like Jimmy, he had a face that gave little away.

"So, they're dangerous. Is that what you're saying?"

Emmerich's eyes locked onto hers, and she felt the full weight of its piercing gravity.

"Ms. Sterling," he said. "Dangerous does not even begin to describe them."

He sat back in his seat without taking his eyes from hers.

"In the shadowed world of corporate power and intrigue, private intelligence agencies prowl in the shadows like ghosts. They are silent and efficient, moving with the stealth and agility of panthers through the urban landscape. They are paid to gather intelligence, to parse data, to uncover secrets that might give their clients an edge in the cutthroat world of business.

"These agencies are the high priests of information, the oracles of the digital age. They are masters of encryption and decryption, of code-breaking and data-mining. They can track a target through a labyrinth of online networks, following the electronic breadcrumbs to their source. Their operatives are the ghosts of the modern world, their movements untraceable, their identities shrouded in secrecy. They operate in the shadows, communicating in code and ciphers, exchanging information on the encrypted channels of the dark web."

He took a deep breath and shook his head at her, his eyes showing a hint of pity.

"In this world of hidden agendas and secret machinations, Ms. Sterling, private intelligence agencies are the eyes and ears of the powerful. They are the guardians of the corporate fortress, the gatekeepers of the digital domain. And they are always watching, Ms. Sterling, always listening, always ready to strike."

He frowned at her.

"You can't go snooping around Viox Genomics or any other major donor to the senator's campaign," he said.

She shrugged.

"Why would they care if they have nothing to hide?" she asked.

He gave a slow, seeping, exasperated sigh.

"It doesn't matter," he said. "Maybe they are all perfectly innocent in this situation. But they also have secrets. Many of them, much, much worse than the murder of a single college student, I assure you. And they will not tolerate you snooping into their business. They will leverage their association with a private intelligence agency, and you will be found in your apartment dead of a drug overdose. The police will say, 'But she had no history of drug use.' And then they will shrug and say, 'It seems you can never really know a person,'" as they zip your corpse up inside a body bag."

They both sat quietly for a while. The place was beginning to fill as the sky brightened outside. The griddle hissed, and the toaster clenched. Knives and forks scraped against plates, while guests muttered and coughed. Tracy said nothing as she stared into Emmerich's eyes.

At last, he shrugged and reached into his pocket. He withdrew several dollar bills and stood.

"Do yourself a favor," he said as he tossed the money on the table. "Stop digging around where you shouldn't and just find someone to pin this on. A jealous boyfriend. An obsessive customer from the gentlemen's club. Use your contacts to point the police in that direction and away from the senator. Collect the rest of your money, and then go on your way."

She looked up at him without speaking.

"Don't forget who is paying you," he said as he turned toward the door. "Please do stay in touch."

Tracy watched as he left the diner without looking back. She sat alone amid the noisy morning chatter and clanking dishes for a few moments longer while her mind digested his words. After a while, she stood up, left the diner and drove back to her apartment.

When she arrived, she found Jimmy still hunched over the laptop, his eyes looking red as he greeted her with a frown.

"What's wrong?" he asked.

She shook her head.

"Nothing. Except for the smell."

Her eyes traveled down to see that he had shed his shoes. There was a hole in one of his black socks, and his big toe jutted out like a great calloused thumb.

"Sorry," he said. "It helps me focus."

She tossed her keys on the table.

"It's fine."

He frowned at her as she sat down in a chair.

"What happened?"

She shook her head.

"Nothing. Have you found anything interesting?"

He raised his eyebrows.

"You might say that."

She perked up in her seat.

"Show me."

He turned back toward the laptop and rewound the video footage. Then, he looked at her and pointed to the screen.

"Do you know this guy?" asked Jimmy.

Tracy looked at the video footage and watched quietly as Dana crossed the room to talk to a man. She leaned in close and squinted at the screen where the two sat together at one of the high-top tables.

Tracy stood up and looked at Jimmy.

"That's Thomas."

Jimmy furrowed his eyebrows.

"Who?"

She put a hand to her forehead.

"He's the senator's campaign manager."

Jimmy turned back to the footage.

"Really?"

They both watched Dana and Thomas chat, while men flowed around their table as they hurried toward the stage where a fresh dancer was plying her luscious wares.

"This is not their first meaning," Jimmy said as he pointed a finger at the screen. "You can tell by their body language."

Tracy nodded.

"What is he giving her?"

Jimmy squinted at the screen.

"Looks like an envelope."

Sure enough, Thomas slid a small envelope across the table. Tracy watched as Dana snatched it up. And then the two parted, and Thomas headed for the door.

"Son of a bitch," said Tracy.

Jimmy pushed back in his chair and looked up at her.

"This is your prime suspect right here."

Tracy looked at him with a skeptical eye.

"I don't know," she said. "I met the guy. He doesn't seem like the type of person to slit someone's throat."

Jimmy shrugged.

"They come in lots of different packaging." He pointed at the screen again. "Whatever the case, he's hiding something. My guess is your senator was having an affair with this girl, and his campaign manager was paying to keep it quiet. Then, maybe she started asking for more money. So, he pays someone to kill her. Solve the problem."

Tracy sat down in a chair.

"That all makes sense," she said. "But it doesn't explain why he'd hire me."

Jimmy frowned at the laptop, where Thomas's image sat frozen on the screen.

"I don't know," he said. "I suppose someone could have killed her on the senator's behalf. Like I said before, these special interests love to get dirt on politicians and then use it as leverage. Then again, it could have just as easily been some random weirdo from the club. A horny stalker who fell in love with a dancer. Maybe she rejected him one too many times."

He leaned forward and pointed at the screen.

"But whatever's really going on, we know one thing for sure. This Thomas guy knows something, and you need to find out what it is. Otherwise, you got jack shit."

Tracy looked at the screen and studied the frozen image, her mind sorting through every available option and all the potential outcomes.

"You're right," she said.

Jimmy looked up at her.

"So. What are you gonna do?"

She looked at the screen and took a deep breath.

"I'm going to get some sleep," she said. "And then, I'm going to go to the senator's mansion and find out what he knows."

Jimmy looked up at her.

"You sure about that?" he asked. "I'm all for the direct approach. But if he did kill this girl or at least had something to do with it, you could be in danger. Maybe it's better to play things close to the vest."

She shrugged.

"It's not like he's going to have me killed inside the senator's mansion."

Jimmy pursed his lips.

"Whatever you say, kid."

Tracy flashed him a look and pointed at the laptop.

"Just keep going through the footage, if you don't mind," she said. "Wake me if you find anything else." She put a hand on her hip. "And don't call me kid."

Jimmy gave her a mock salute.

"Yes, ma'am."

He watched as she made her way to the bedroom and shut the door behind her. Then, he gave a yawn of his own and turned his attention back to the laptop.

Chapter 10

They day was mostly gone by the time Tracy's sleep finally broke, and she cursed herself as she wrestled free from the tangle of bedsheets. With a stumble, she got to her feet and dressed before charging out into the living room, where she found Jimmy snoring on the couch.

With a hard poke, she jabbed him in the ribs. He gave a snort and opened his eyes, which were still heavily webbed red.

"Do you know what time it is?" she asked.

He looked up at her and blinked, his eyes wild, hair a snarling disaster.

"No."

She pointed to the clock on the wall.

"It's 6 pm."

He sat up and coughed.

"So?"

She held her hands out to her side.

"So, we've got work to do."

He rubbed his head and looked around.

"Where's the coffee?"

She put her hands on her hips.

"Did you find anything in the security footage?"

He looked up at her.

"To be honest, I fell asleep shortly after you did."

She shook her head.

"What happened to sleep is for the weak?"

He shrugged.

"Fatigue makes cowards of us all."

She sighed.

"Brilliant. Do you have a book of these snappy little quotes?"

He frowned and watched as she went into the bathroom. About 30 minutes later, a different woman came out, this one, neat and dressed and much easier on the eyes.

Jimmy watched as she walked over to the table and collected her gun.

"You stay here and go through the rest of the security footage. I'm going to go talk to the senator's campaign manager and find out what he knows."

She slipped the pistol into its holster under her jacket and headed for the door.

"Tracy," said Jimmy as he watched her with weary eyes.

She paused and looked back at him.

"Watch your back."

She shook her head.

"Just keep looking over the video. I'll be back in a few hours."

There was barely any color left on the horizon, when Tracy arrived at the senator's estate. In the fading light, she followed the narrow gravel road that wound away from the main highway. On either side, tall trees stretched high above her car, their branches clawing at the soft pink clouds as if to siphon away the failing sun.

She nervously tapped her fingers on the steering wheel, gravel crunching beneath her tires as she turned off the main road and rolled up the long driveway. Just ahead, the grand wrought-iron gate shut away the senator's estate. Flanking the side of the barrier was the brick guard shack, where a single silhouetted occupant watched her from a small window that flickered with warm yellow light. As her car approached, the security man stepped out into the early evening, his hand resting firmly on the gun in his holster. Casting an appraising glance towards Tracy, he firmed his mouth and frowned.

"How can I help you this evening?" he asked as he lit her face with a flashlight.

Tracy squinted up at him.

"Tracy Sterling," she said. "I'm expected."

The security man looked a little confused.

"I wasn't told."

Tracy raised her eyebrows.

"Well, then, get on your phone and confirm it. I'm in a hurry."

The security man glared at her and backed away a few steps. Without taking his eyes off her, he slipped out his phone and gave it a few taps. Then, he held it to his ear and waited. Tracy raised a hand to block the searing beam of the flashlight.

"You mind taking that light off me?"

The security man ignored her and began speaking into the phone. Soon, the conversation devolved into a repetitive series of "yes, sirs." And then, the man hung up his phone, returned to his little shed and opened the wrought-iron gate. Tracy glared at him as she rolled forward, but he did not return her gaze.

As she pushed closer to the mansion, an unease festered within her chest, and when she looked into her rearview mirror, she saw the gate closing as if to seal away her retreat.

Moments later, she rolled beneath the canopy of cherry blossom trees, and one of the lower branches raked the top of her car. With a jolting start, she flinched at the sound of the shrieking metal and then scolded herself for how jittery she'd become since her encounter with Vincent two nights before.

Steadying her nerves with a few slow breaths, she parked and climbed the steps, a touch of apprehension still nagging at her mind as she approached the stately mansion.

Shaking these feelings away, she gave the doorbell a poke and then grimaced a little, when Emmerich opened the door.

"Ms. Sterling," he said with his low, whispery voice.

Tracy looked up at the thin man's harsh, angular face, which seemed less human than ever in the diminished light.

"Emmerich," she said with a polite smile.

The man's vivid eyes burned within the hollows of his skeletal sockets, but he seemed to show no emotion at all.

"You are here to see the senator's campaign manager?"

Tracy nodded.

"That's right."

He raised his eyebrows and stared down at her.

"I am your primary point of contact. Was that not made clear the other night?"

Tracy nodded.

"Yes. I understand. I just need to clarify some things with Thomas. It's part of the investigation. Unless that creates a problem for you."

Emmerich watched her for a moment,

"No," he said. "Of course not. But do keep me informed on your progress. Assuming, of course, that you ever make any."

Before she could reply, he turned away and moved into the foyer. She followed him inside and stood beneath the great chandelier, which glittered above them like a crystal sun.

"Thomas is waiting for you," he said with his gravelly hiss of a voice. "I will show you the way."

They crossed the marble floor and passed into the same long curving hallway from her first visit. But on this night, the surroundings seemed especially ominous, and Tracy found herself ill at ease, as the faces in the tapestries gazed down with their soulless eyes.

Emmerich's long legs seemed to move in slow motion with every step. But he made good ground. And Tracy had to hurry to keep up with the lanky man. At last, he paused and gestured toward a door.

"He is waiting inside," he said.

He stepped back and watched her.

"Thanks," said Tracy.

He gave a nod and narrowed his glittering eyes.

"Do keep me informed," he said. "We should be working together as much as possible."

She gave a nod, and the man walked away, his large feet squelching against the thick, burgundy carpet as he vanished around the curving edge of the hallway.

Tracy exhaled a long breath and then opened the door. Inside, Thomas stood by a small bar, a drink in his hand as he forced a polite smile.

"Hello, Ms. Sterling. How was your drive?"

Tracy entered and shut the door behind her.

"Fine."

He gave a polite smile and nodded.

"Can I get you a drink?"

"No," she said.

He nodded.

"And how was your encounter with Emmerich?"

Tracy shrugged.

"I don't think he likes me very much."

Thomas nodded.

"I know the feeling."

Thomas started to say something else, but she held a hand up.

"Let's just cut to the chase here, ok?"

He raised his eyebrows.

"Alright," he said as he sat in a chair. "What would you like to discuss?"

Tracy folded her arms.

"Well, let's start with your relationship with Dana Brockers."

He looked somewhat startled as he sat back in his seat.

"I can assure you I had no relationship with Ms. Brockers."

Tracy frowned.

"Well, you knew her somehow."

"What makes you say that?" he asked.

"Because you met with her the night of her murder. I saw you on the security footage."

He shifted in his seat.

"It was my understanding that the venue does not have security cameras in place."

Tracy shrugged.

"Turns out they lie a lot. Now, quit bullshitting me and tell me what the fuck is going on."

He put a hand up.

"Just relax."

Tracy narrowed her eyes.

"I'll relax when you tell me what's going on."

He sighed.

"It's true. I did meet with her the night of her murder. But there was really nothing strange about that."

"And why is that?" asked Tracy.

He shrugged.

"Because I met with her every month.

"Why?" asked Tracy. "Were you having an affair with her?"

He looked genuinely offended.

"No. Of course not."

She turned her palms upward.

"Then why?"

114

He sighed.

"I was delivering money."

"Money?" asked Tracy. "Why?"

He frowned.

"I'm afraid this is where things get somewhat sordid."

Tracy sat back in her seat.

"Ah, I think I understand," she said. "The senator was having an affair with Dana, and you were delivering hush money to keep her quiet about it."

He scratched his jaw.

"Not exactly."

"No?" she asked. "Then, why would you be giving her money on a regular basis? What other explanation could there be?"

His face took on an apologetic expression.

"I'm sorry. I'm really not supposed to say."

Tracy gave a false smile.

"That's fine. But it's only a matter of time before the police catch on."

He furrowed his brow.

"Why? Don't you have the security video? Why don't you just give it to me? And we can keep this between us. You did sign an NDA, after all."

She shook her head.

"Even if I agreed to that, you'd be a fool to believe other copies don't exist. Especially considering where I got the footage. Hell, my guess is you'll be delivering envelopes to the owner of that place pretty soon. Unless, of course, you want to stop playing games and give me the information I need to help you and the senator out of this jam."

He swallowed.

"Hold on," he said as he stood.

She watched as he pulled his cell phone from his pocket and turned away. He tapped it a few times and held it to his ear. Tracy watched as he mumbled to someone on the other end, his words low and garbled as he took a few steps from her.

After about a minute, he hung up the phone and turned around.

"Senator Jenkins is coming down."

Tracy raised her eyebrows.

"Really?"

Thomas nodded.

"He'll be here shortly."

Tracy gave a nod and watched as Thomas poured himself another drink. Moments later, the door swung open, and the senator stepped inside. Both Thomas and Tracy stood as he entered the room and looked it over, blue eyes beaming beneath his neatly parted salt-and-pepper hair. He gave Thomas a nod and then turned to Tracy.

"Hello, Ms. Sterling," he said. "I'm glad to finally meet you."

He was tall and handsome, and he offered her his hand like it was a reward.

"Likewise," she said as they clasped palms.

He gave her hand a courteous shake and then nodded to Thomas, who turned to pour him a drink. Then, he sat in a large leather chair and gestured for Tracy to do the same in the chair across from him.

"I'm sorry it's taken so long for us to meet," he said. "I've been quite busy of late."

Tracy shrugged.

"I understand."

The senator's face turned somber as Thomas pushed a drink into his hand.

"I was very sad to hear about Ms. Brockers. It was a tragic turn of events. And, sadly, unsurprising."

Tracy raised her eyebrows.

"Why's that?"

"As you know," said Thomas, "we were expecting this outcome, Ms. Sterling."

Tracy nodded.

"Yes," she said. "But why?"

The senator sipped his drink and peered at her over the glass.

"As I told you before," said Thomas. "We're unable to divulge every detail. I'm sorry."

Tracy nodded.

"Sure," she said. "Well, I'd suggest you start planning for a big police investigation, complete with wall-to-wall media coverage."

The senator set his glass on a small wooden end table and crossed his legs. He regarded Tracy with a patient smile, his face calm and effortlessly composed.

"I'm paying you to prevent that," he said.

Tracy gave a little chuckle.

116

"You're asking me to work a miracle," she said. "Listen, this isn't something you can just throw money at to make it go away. Money helps, yes. But I can't do this job without all the facts. No one could. It's like trying to diffuse a bomb in the dark. It doesn't matter whether I'm any good at this or not. I could be Sherlock fucking Holmes, and I'm telling you, there is no way this ends well for you unless you come clean and give me all the facts."

The senator lowered his eyebrows and frowned at her thoughtfully, while Thomas plopped down in his chair and began chewing his thumbnail.

"Alright," said the senator. "I'll answer your questions."

He gave a polite little smile, his face a mask of satisfaction, as if he had been the one to suggest the turn toward honesty. Tracy stared into his eyes, the bluest she had ever seen.

"Were you having an affair with Dana Brockers?"

Thomas straightened in his chair.

"Senator, you don't have to answer that. You don't have to answer any of her questions. She agreed to that when she signed the deal."

Senator Jenkins raised a hand to silence him.

"Thank you, Thomas," he said. "But I will answer."

He turned toward Tracy.

"No," he said. "I was not."

Tracy raised her eyebrows.

"With all due respect, it's hard to accept that. An affair would help explain a lot of this. Why should I believe you? It seems like something you would want to hide."

The senator pursed his lips and watched her, while Thomas squirmed in his chair.

"Senator," said the campaign manager. "I recommend that we end this conversation now before things get too complicated. I can handle this on your behalf."

Jenkins shushed him with a finger. He stared at Tracy and cocked his head to the side.

"You want to know why you should believe me?"

Tracy shrugged.

"This is an extremely bizarre situation," she said. "You hired me to prove your innocence in a murder that had yet to occur. You were clearly familiar with Dana Brockers, and you thought you had reason to believe she would be killed. That makes me think she was

117

probably blackmailing you. And with an election on the horizon, what better reason to blackmail a candidate than an extramarital affair?"

Thomas grimaced and looked away, while the senator narrowed his eyes a little and sat back in his seat.

"Alright," he said. "I'll answer your question. The reason you should believe that I didn't have an affair with Dana is because she was my daughter."

Tracy's eyebrows shot up.

"Your daughter?"

The senator started to speak, but Thomas interrupted.

"We're not sure," he said. "We think she may be."

Tracy shook her head and assessed the two men anew.

"Wait a minute," she said. "You're going to need to catch me up."

The senator looked back at Thomas.

"Where should we start?" he asked the campaign manager.

"Start at the fucking beginning," said Tracy.

Both men turned, their faces showing surprise at her coarse tone.

"Listen," she said as she eyed each man. "A young woman is dead. And there's no way I'm going to be able to clear you of this unless I have the whole story. So, let's quit screwing around and tell me everything I need to know."

The senator frowned at Thomas and then turned back to Tracy.

"Fine," he said. "But everything I tell you tonight is to remain private. If even a word of this gets out, my people will ruin you. Do you understand?"

Tracy shook her head with exasperation.

"Get on with it," she said.

The senator stood up from his chair and looked at Thomas. As if some telepathic exchange had taken place, the campaign manager sprung to his feet and crossed the room. He stopped at a small liquor cabinet and withdrew a bottle of scotch. The senator waited for Thomas to push a glass into his hand. Then, he took a long slug and exhaled with a hiss.

"You're instincts are pretty good, Ms. Sterling. This whole thing did start with an extramarital affair. But it happened a long time ago. Maybe 20 years. Maybe longer."

He took another drink and gestured to Thomas for a refill.

"I had a short affair with Alicia Brockers. That would be Dana's mother, apparently. It was a very brief affair, maybe a month or two. Anyway, when it ended, I almost forgot about it. Until she contacted my people and started demanding money. Apparently, she had evidence of our encounters. Photos and videos or whatnot. Anyway, she threatened to go to the press if I didn't compensate her."

He shrugged at Tracy.

"So, we started making payments. Every month for almost a year. And she kept her silence. Right up until the day they found her in a quarry with a knife in her eye."

Tracy raised her eyebrows.

"I checked into Dana's family, and the report said her mother died by suicide."

The senator looked at Thomas, who gave an almost embarrassed shrug.

"We had some connections with the police at the time. And we used them to push the detectives toward that conclusion. It wasn't our proudest moment, but we felt it was in everyone's best interest if the case was closed."

Tracy's lip curled slightly as she thought of her father and Bradley, and all the corruption that had driven her from the police force.

"You mean you covered the senator's tracks."

Thomas pointed a finger at her.

"Senator Jenkins had nothing to do with her death," he said. "Not directly, anyway."

Tracy narrowed her eyes at the senator.

"And then," she said. "Two decades later, you get a call from Dana Brockers, and the cycle repeats itself."

The senator shrugged.

"You're good," he said. "About six months ago, Dana called my people and said she was the illegitimate daughter of myself and Alicia Brockers. She then threatened to go public unless she received monetary compensation, which we began paying monthly almost immediately."

Tracy looked at Thomas.

"This is why you were meeting with her at Dougie's?"

The campaign manager shrugged.

"Same day, every month."

Tracy shook her head.

"Well, then," she said. "If everything you've told me is true, you will definitely be the primary suspect. The police will either try to finger you or prove that you hired Dana's killer. Even if they can't prove any of it, the media will have a field day with the story."

Both men nodded.

"Unless you can prove otherwise."

Tracy shook her head.

"How?" she asked. "Can you give me something else to go on? Who do you think is behind the murders? One of your enemies? One of your contributors?"

Both men shrugged.

"Possibly," said Thomas.

"Possibly," Tracy repeated to herself.

She shook her head.

"What about Emmerich?" she asked.

The men exchanged looks and frowned.

"No," said the senator. "I know he has the look. But his loyalty is based on a paycheck. He's not going to kill someone on my behalf. Not unless I paid him to do it."

Tracy looked at him and narrowed her eyes.

"What about him?" she asked as she gestured toward Thomas.

"Me?" asked the campaign manager.

Tracy shrugged.

"How deep does his loyalty go? What would he do to keep your name out of the headlines?"

Thomas stood up.

"Not kill someone," he said with iron in his voice.

The senator put a hand on his arm.

"Ms. Sterling, I can appreciate what you're doing, but I can assure you my people had nothing to do with this. And neither did I."

Tracy frowned at both men.

"Well, who then?" she asked. "Give me the names of your enemies. Who holds a grudge against you? Who needs leverage over you to make you dance to their tune?"

Both men frowned.

"I can give you some names. But I can't have you poking your nose around the wrong places. That wouldn't be good for us or you."

Tracy turned her palms upward.

"Then, what do you want me to do?" she asked. "You're handicapping me and then asking me to work a miracle."

Thomas sat back down in his chair and looked at her.

"We don't necessarily need you to solve the case," he said. "We just need you to help aim the investigation away from the senator."

"How?" asked Tracy. "I'm not a cop anymore."

"But you have connections in the police department," said the senator.

She looked at the men and sat quietly for a moment.

"I'm not going to frame someone to protect you," she said at last.

"No," said Thomas. "Of course not. Just find some suitable suspects and feed them to your connections. Give them something to go on, so they won't waste time with the senator. What we want to avoid most of all is a public investigation."

Tracy narrowed her eyes at both men.

"And whoever is really behind all this," she said, "what if they decide to go public? What if they pull the rug out from under you?"

The senator shrugged.

"I've been a puppet most my life, Ms. Sterling," he said. "This is nothing new. The real problem is the police. You know as well as I do that things have changed. The entire precinct has undergone a massive corruption scandal, thanks mostly to you. We've lost our connections, and the department is run by a boy scout who would love nothing more than to tear down the establishment. I need you to give the cops some red meat, so they'll point their noses in a different direction. This girl was a stripper at a veritable drug den. There have to be some suitable people of interest. Dig into the potential candidates and feed the details to your connections within the police. We're paying you a lot of money for this. And frankly, I'm not sure we're getting a return on our investment. Not yet, at least."

Tracy glared at the senator, who responded with a casual shrug.

"Judge me all you want, Ms. Sterling," he said. "I made a mistake. I was unfaithful to my wife. But that is where my sins end. At least with regard to Dana and her mother. I didn't kill anyone. And I didn't ask anyone to do it for me. Whatever you think of me, I didn't have the power to prevent their deaths."

Tracy half chuckled, even as she pinned him with a fierce glare.

"Power?" she said. "You're all about power. Isn't that what this is really about? Isn't that what everything is about?"

He sneered at her.

"You know nothing," he said. "You think you do. But you are just a babe in the deep, dark woods. When I first got into politics, I was naive, like you. I had big hopes. I was going to change the world. But I learned quickly. They made me learn quickly. I am just a cog in a great machine. There are interests to serve. And they do not give you a choice."

"Who are you talking about?" asked Tracy.

The senator raised his glass as if toasting to her health.

"The rich and the powerful," he said. "The ones pulling strings anonymously as they stand behind the curtain. The people who make the world."

He downed the rest of his drink and set the empty glass on a table.

"This will be our last meeting," he said. "I'm counting on you to earn your money."

He nodded to Thomas before turning away and walking out the door. When he was gone, Tracy looked at Thomas, who had an apologetic frown on his face.

"I'm sorry," he said. "He's not himself tonight. There's some tension between him and Ms. Jenkins."

"Oh, I'll bet," said Tracy.

Thomas shrugged.

"I'm sorry we can't be of more help. We're really just as clueless as you are."

Tracy stood up.

"Well, if anything pops into your head —something you forgot to mention, perhaps —give me a call. I know you like to keep things close to the vest, but you're really only hurting the senator's interests, whether you realize it or not."

Thomas stood up and nodded.

"Of course," he said. "I understand. I'll let you know if anything comes to mind."

She gave him an uncertain look as he approached the door.

"Let me show you out," he said.

When she stepped through the front door, the night was full bore, and the grounds seemed to glow green beneath a pale sliver of a moon.

As the door shut behind her, Tracy stepped out into the drive and turned to look back at the mansion. One of the second-story windows was lit by a soft amber light, and in that window, a middle-aged woman looked down. Although the features were indistinct from such a distance, Tracy recognized her from the television as the senator's wife. She raised her chin to get a better look, and the woman let the curtains fall as she backed away from sight.

Tracy let her eyes fall from the window to the front door. Then, she turned away and walked to her car just as her phone began burbling in her pocket. She slipped it out and checked the number before answering the call.

"Yeah," she said as she sat in her car.

"Where are you now?" asked Jimmy.

"I'm just leaving the senator's place," she said. "Why? What's up?"

"I've been digging deeper into the security footage from Dougie's."

"Yeah?" she said as she pulled away from the great house.

"Yeah," he said. "I'll meet you at your apartment in about an hour. There's something you need to see."

Chapter 11

Tony stood outside the drug store, his hands in his pockets as customers came and went. With an affable demeanor, he threw polite smiles to people as they passed, his face bruised and swollen beneath the big white bandage smothering his fractured nose.

A man in a suit flinched at the sight of him as he entered the store. A woman yanked her young daughter closer as she hurried to follow. And all the while, Tony smiled, a faint tune on his whistling lips as he tapped his shoe against the broken sidewalk.

At last, an old woman exited the store and paused before the small metal trash can positioned just out front of the store. Tony held his breath and watched as she discarded an empty bottle of water and a crumpled receipt. He watched and waited until she moved toward the parking lot. Then, he looked all around before plunging his hands into the trash.

He rooted through something slick and grimaced a little before withdrawing the soiled piece of paper. With a sickly expression, he approached the side of the building and wiped the glistening ooze from his skin. Then, he held the receipt up and looked it over. It said corn chips, denture adhesive and stool softener. Shaking his head, he tossed the strip of paper aside and leaned back against the building.

That was the ninth dead end so far, and his bladder was begging for an end to the mission. But just as he was about to give up, a beautiful woman exited the store. Tony shrunk back against the brick wall and froze as if to make himself invisible. Then, he watched as the woman tossed her receipt into the trashcan and made her way across the parking lot.

Tony watched and waited, his tongue running over his lips as he stared at the trash can. When the coast was clear, he hurried over and reached back into the bin, withdrawing the receipt, which had already turned moist and revolting by the mysterious mucus within.

Without pausing, he dropped to his knees and wiped the paper against the sidewalk. When it was suitably dry, he held it up and grinned. With an exuberant bounce, he hopped to his feet and spun toward the door, where the woman and child from before stood watching. Each regarded him like something that had peeled off the bottom of a shoe, and he rewarded their disdain with a chivalrous bow.

"Let's go, Cindy," hissed the woman as the two rushed past him.

Tony watched them hurry away. Then, he shoved the receipt into his pocket and hurried inside. With a quick, deliberate pace, he crossed to the back of the store and made his way through the aisles. He held a finger to his lip and scanned the shelves until he found his target. With a grin, he plucked the product from the shelf and hurried toward the register.

He waited in line a few minutes, his nose aching beneath his bandaged face. At last, the line thinned to nothing, and he took a position before the cashier. This was a large woman who regarded Tony with a set of hawkish hazel eyes.

"Can I help you?" she asked.

Tony dropped the merchandise on the counter.

"I want to return this," he said.

The woman picked up the bottle of beauty cream.

"What's wrong with it?" she asked.

Tony shrugged.

"I bought it for my wife, and she said it was the wrong brand."

The woman eyed him and frowned.

"Why don't you exchange it for the right brand?"

Tony shrugged.

"You don't carry the right brand."

The woman grunted and set the bottle of cream back down.

"Do you have a receipt?"

Tony reached into his pocket and retrieved the slip of paper.

"Here you go."

He slapped the paper down on the counter like a winning lottery ticket, his face brightening as he smiled at the cashier. Her lip curled as she assessed the receipt, which glistened beneath the bright fluorescent lights like something eternally wet.

"What happened to it?" she asked.

Tony shrugged.

"It got mixed up with some trash."

The woman frowned at him and then looked back down at the receipt. As if pulling a sticker from the countertop, she peeled away the strip of paper and held it up to her face. She squinted at it and then looked at Tony, who continued to smile back in a way that made her shiver on the inside.

At last, she set the receipt aside and cracked open the register. Minutes later, Tony walked outside with $85 in cash, his face bright and proud as the sun warmed his skin.

And then he felt the big hand curl around his arm.

"Hello, Tony," said a deep voice.

Tony turned and swallowed.

"Shit," he whispered.

Jimmy looked down at the small man, his face expressionless as ever. But within his eyes burned a fiery hate that made Tony's bladder spasm.

"We need to have a little talk," said another voice.

Tony turned his head to see Tracy approaching.

"Shit," he whispered again.

"Come on," said Jimmy.

They led Tony around to the backside of the drug store and set him before a big rusty dumpster. Tony rubbed his arm and looked at the two of them, his body flinching away from Jimmy, who eyed him like a snake watching a mouse.

"Relax," said Tracy. "He's not going to hurt you."

"Bullshit," said Tony. "He hurts people all the time."

"Well," she said as she looked at his bandaged face. "You may have a point."

Tony licked his lips and eyed each of them in turn.

"What the hell is this about?" he asked.

"It's about you, Tony," said Tracy.

"Me?"

She nodded.

"You and Dana Brockers."

126

She watched his face, but if she expected a response, a tell of any kind, his practiced facade left her disappointed.

"The girl from Dougie's?" he asked. "I told you, I didn't see nothin." He gestured toward Jimmy. "This big motherfucker grabbed me before I could see anything."

Jimmy swelled before him.

"Drop the act, you piece of shit," he said.

Tony stumbled back a step and put his hands up in surrender.

"What act?" he asked. "I don't know what you two are talking about. Honest."

Tracy took in a slow breath and shook her head.

"Stop, Tony," she said. "We've seen the security footage from the other night. I sent you into that place to watch her, and the moment you entered, you immediately walked right up to her and whispered in her ear."

Tony's face assumed an expression of wounded innocence.

"What? I don't know what you're talking about."

Jimmy flashed his teeth.

"Cut the bullshit," he said as he turned toward Tracy. "This is a waste of time. Just let me beat it out of him."

Tony swallowed hard.

"Okay, okay," he said. "Just wait a second. Yeah, I kind of knew her, I guess. I've been to Dougie's a couple of times. I watched her dance. That's all."

Tracy shook her head.

"No, Tony," she said. "I watched the tape. You knew that girl, and she knew you. It was written on both of your faces."

Tony looked at her as if she'd grown a second head.

"What?" he said. "I don't know what you think you saw, but you're way off base."

Jimmy shook his head and stepped forward.

"That's it," he said as he folded his hand around Tony's wrist.

The small man gave a little yelp as Jimmy spun him around and leveraged his arm behind his back, bringing him face-to-face with Tracy.

"He's gonna break my arm," Tony shrieked.

Tracy assessed him with cold detachment.

"Not if you answer our questions," she said.

Tony grimaced and gasped.

"Okay, okay," he said. "Just let me go."

127

Jimmy looked at Tracy, who gave a nod. Then, he released Tony and stepped back.

"Start talking," he said as he regarded Tony with disgust. "And no more bullshit, or you'll be spitting teeth."

Tony winced as he cradled his arm like a dying child.

"I think he tore something," he said.

Tracy stepped forward and took hold of his chin.

"Focus, Tony," she said. "Tell me what you told Dana that night."

He swallowed and shrugged.

"I told her there was a PI outside. That you had been watching her."

Tracy raised her eyebrows.

"And how did you know her?"

He glanced back at Jimmy, who regarded him with a curl of his lip.

"Tony," said Tracy.

"Alright, alright," he said. "We worked together a few times."

Tracy and Jimmy exchanged looks.

"What do you mean you worked together?" asked Tracy.

Tony shrugged.

"We ran a few cons together."

Tracy furrowed her brow.

"Tony."

"I'm serious," he said. "No bullshit."

Tracy looked at Jimmy again, and he shrugged.

"I guess it's possible," he said. "But I wouldn't trust anything he says."

Tracy looked at Tony and shook her head.

"No," she said. "He'll tell us the truth." She looked into Tony's eyes. "Because if you don't, Jimmy's going to finish with that arm and then start with the other."

Tony swallowed.

"Alright," he said. "I got it."

Tracy frowned at him.

"Start talking," she said. "I want the whole story."

"Sure," he said as he rubbed his arm. "Whatever you say."

He glanced at Jimmy and swallowed. Then, he took in a deep breath, and the words came spilling out, as if he'd been secretly hoping to brag about his exploits all along.

"I met Dana about two years ago," he said. "I was doing pretty good back then. Not like now. Me and this other guy ran this short con on some businessman from out of town and scored big. I was gonna take my cut and skip town. But, you know how it is. That new money started burning a hole in my pocket. Next thing I know, I'm at Dougie's every other night, spending money like there was no tomorrow. That's where I met Dana.

"She was a new addition at the time. And the newest girls are hot items. It's always been that way there. But with that body and that hair, Dana was something different altogether. Everyone was throwing money her way. No one could get enough. Of course, she didn't want anything to do with a guy like me. And I don't blame her. But I had a thing for her, I'm ashamed to say. I know how pathetic it is when guys fall for strippers. But I'm human like all the rest.

"Anyway, I started tipping real heavy to try to get her attention. And it worked. Before I knew it, she started making a big fuss when I came into the place. I looked like a high-roller, and I ran through my cash pretty fast. But that's what it took to hold her interest, so I just kept spending. I couldn't help myself. No one could with her.

"Now, normally, when the money runs out, the girls at that place bat their eyelashes somewhere else. But she had a curious mind, and she wanted to know how a guy like me had fallen into that much cash. I told her most of it had gone into her pockets. Although the truth is a whole helluva lot of it went straight up my nose. Whatever. I got vices like everyone else.

"Anyway, although it's generally against my policy, I ended up telling her the truth. That I was a hustler and a confidence man who ran a few decent-sized rackets every now and then throughout the city. Being that forthcoming, it's something I would never do under normal circumstances. But this girl. You gotta understand. She just looked at you, and she instantly owned you. You never had a chance. No one would."

He looked over at Jimmy.

"Not even him."

Jimmy folded his arms and Tony seemed to flinch a little.

"Get on with it," said Tracy.

"Right," he continued, "So, when I told Dana what I did for a living, she got intrigued. She liked the idea of it. I think she romanticized it in some way. Like the movies. Even though it ain't really like that at all. But she had an idea in her head, and that was it.

129

And in the end, she was really just a junkie like everyone else at that place. For some, it was tits and ass. For others, drugs and booze. For her, it was money and the rush. Adrenaline and cash. It's how she got off. And when she found out what I did, she wanted in."

"Let me tell you, I was blown away. Not only was I going to get to have this beauty by my side a little while longer, my mind was cooking up all kinds of ways I could use her face and body to fleece a mark. And that's what we did. For about a year, we ran up all kinds of scores. And no one was the wiser. Not the cops. Not vincent. Not no one."

Tracy narrowed her eyes.

"How?" she asked.

"How what?" he said.

"How did you run cons together? What exactly did you do?"

He shrugged.

"All kinds of shit," he said. "Some well-dressed rich guy would come into Dougie's, and she would make the connection. She'd pay him a lot of attention. Make him feel special. Like a big important man. Get him excited. Make him fall in love. There'd be private dances and little conversations at his table. During which she would make it clear she had a thing for high rollers who had the means and the balls to risk big bets. She said it got her juices flowing. If you know what I mean."

Tracy's lip curled.

"Keep going," she said.

Tony shrugged.

"Anyway, at this point, she'd turn it off. Point herself at someone else. And wait until the mark started to fume with jealousy. Then, just as he was about to lose hope, she'd re-engage and start selling the con."

Jimmy shook his head.

"What was the con?" he asked.

"She'd tell him there was a place on the south side. An old warehouse where guys ran an illegal gambling operation. She'd ask the mark to take her. Sometimes, they'd say no. But when she started batting those eyelashes, most said yes."

Tracy sat back and shook her head.

"But it was really you running this place. Is that it?"

Tony shrugged.

"Me and a few other guys," he said. "But we made it look good. When you got a steady supply of rich, clueless rubes and a girl like

Dana to deliver them, it's not hard to find other professionals like me who want in. And the ones I work with know their business."

"So, we made a pretty elaborate setup. In the business, we call it a big store. It takes a lot of planning and investment. But the payoff is nice."

He gave a prideful shrug, and Jimmy shook his head.

"Listen, you little bastard—" he began, but Tracy raised her hand.

"Just wait," she said.

Jimmy firmed his mouth and folded his arms, while Tracy turned back toward Tony.

"Give me the short version, Tony. ok?"

He eyed Jimmy with fear.

"Sure," he said. "Well, the gist of it is we set up a little underground gaming club with some roulette, poker, a sportsbook with only horse racing. Dana would bring in the marks, and we'd let them win a little. Get their juices flowing, so they felt like a big shot in front of the girl. Then, a few days later, she'd bring one to me, and I'd tell them about a racket I had going. How I had one of the games rigged. And she'd convince them to go in with us for a big score. We'd let them win a little while, and she'd work their ego until they put up a nice fat wager. Then, we'd slam the door on them and take them for a big score."

Tracy shook her head.

"And then you'd cool them off, so they didn't get to the cops," said Tracy.

Tony raised his eyebrows.

"So, you do get how this works," he said. "Not just go to the cops, though. These days, a mark is liable to shoot you if you don't cool him down. Sometimes, it's a real problem. But it was easy in this case because even if they suspected something, none of the marks were gonna go into Dougie's and start accusing one of the dancers of running a con on them. Not with Vincent around. That'd be a good way to get beat to death. And it didn't matter anyway because we always had some guys in uniform come bust the big store up right after we made our final play. And the mark was just happy to get the hell out of there without getting arrested. We never saw any of them again. It worked like clockwork. We all got a cut, and Dana's cut was biggest because we couldn't have done it without her."

Tracy narrowed her eyes.

131

"Guys in uniform?" she asked. "Who?"

He shook his head.

"Not real cops," he said. "Just some guys in cosplay. Although we could have easily got a few real cops. I promise you. But we were running this thing on the cheap."

Tracy felt her lip curl again.

"How does all this relate to the senator?" she asked.

Tony eyed Jimmy for a moment and nervously licked his lips.

"Well," he said. "During the course of our partnership, Dana let slip that her mom used to screw a senator. And a light bulb went off in my head."

Tracy sighed and shook her head.

"Oh, Tony, you piece of shit," she said. "You convinced her to extort money from his campaign by pretending to be his illegitimate daughter."

Tony shrugged.

"Hey," he said. "It wasn't like we were burning babies. For all I know, she really was this guy's daughter. Based on her age, the math lines up. And she told me she never knew who her real dad was. The way I see it, if he was her dad, he owed her the money. And if he wasn't, he brought this on himself by fucking around on his wife in the first place."

He shrugged.

"Anyway, Dana didn't have qualms. I'll tell you that. It was all a game to her. And she liked the idea of being a senator's daughter. So, we worked his people for a few months. And everything was going just fine. Until you showed up and told me to keep an eye on her. That's when I knew the jig was up. So, I gave her a head's up. And then, your friend there grabbed me."

Tracy sat back and thought for a moment, while Jimmy frowned at the small man.

"Tell me something else, Tony," said Tracy. "The senator's people, do they know about you?"

Tony shook his head.

"No way. They dealt with Dana exclusively. I was only the architect. And I only took a small cut."

Tracy thought for a moment, while Tony fidgeted before Jimmy's gaze.

"Wait here a second," she said as she pulled Jimmy aside.

132

She led him several feet away, while he continued to watch Tony with violent intent. When they were out of earshot, she leaned in and started whispering.

"I've got an idea."

Jimmy stared over her shoulder, his eyes glistening with hate.

"Jimmy," she said. "Listen."

He looked down at her, and his face returned to its normal expressionless state.

"I'm listening," he said.

"The way I see it," she began, "Jenkins' people hired me because they knew Dana Brockers was going to die. They knew it the moment she started extorting him. And the reason they knew it was because the same thing happened with her mom."

Jimmy nodded.

"I'm with you," he said. "But nothing has changed, Tracy. Even if this piece of shit is actually being truthful—which, I'm telling you, is not likely—it doesn't help us much. It doesn't change our pool of suspects. If anything, it complicates things. Now we have the senator's people, Vincent's people, hired killers working on behalf of one of the senator's supporters, and a possible mark who wants to get even with a stripper that conned him out of money. Lots of hypothetical people with very compelling motives. There's nothing we can do."

Tracy shook her head.

"None of that matters because now we have the key."

Jimmy's eyes followed her outstretched arm, which was pointing at Tony.

"You're shitting me," said Jimmy. "He's the fucking key?"

Tracy nodded.

'Absolutely. Now that we have Tony, we can recreate the entire thing. We'll just have him call the senator's people and tell them he was working with Dana. He'll say he knows she was the senator's daughter. And he'll threaten to tell the press unless he gets the same deal she got. They'll instantly agree and start paying him off. We'll keep a close eye on him, monitor the payments. At some point, the killer will try to take him out too. And we'll catch him in the act. It's all right here. Easy as pie."

Jimmy glanced over at Tony and thought for a moment. Then, he looked back at Tracy and rubbed his whiskered jaw.

"Three things," he said. "First, you're talking about working with one of the least trustworthy people I've ever met. He'll be looking to skip town every chance he gets. If we let our guard down for even a second, he's gone. So, that means one of us will be living with him at all times, regardless of how long it takes."

She started to speak, but he stopped her.

"Second," he continued, "You need to consider that what you're talking about is illegal. Extortion is a crime, and our involvement would make this whole endeavor a conspiracy to commit this crime. And, you should also bear in mind that in this instance, the crime would be extortion of a U.S. senator, which would be a federal offense."

Tracy shook her head.

"I was hired by the senator to prove his innocence. I wasn't told what I could and couldn't do. I can stand in court and testify that the senator essentially condoned my actions by hiring me in the first place."

Jimmy frowned at her.

"I don't know about that," he said. "I have my doubts, but I'm not a lawyer. But despite your theory, it's a big risk in my opinion. But it's not the risk that worries me. My bigger concern is the third issue."

Tracy raised her eyebrows.

"Which is?"

Jimmy sighed.

"Which is," he began, "are you really sure you want to actually catch this person?"

Tracy furrowed her brows.

"What do you mean?"

He frowned at her as if summoning the patience to reason with a child.

"Tracy," he said. "I admire your passion. I always have. But you're not seeing all the angles. What if this Emmerich guy is right? What if the killer really is one of these private intelligence agencies? If that's the case, it means Dana was taken out by professional hitmen. Someone working on behalf of a billion-dollar corporation with the ability to bribe cops, hire the world's best lawyers, and give your home address to more hired hitmen."

Tracy started to roll her eyes.

"Damn it, Tracy, I'm serious," Jimmy said. "You're not a cop anymore. You don't have the same protection you once had. You're just a civilian now, like everyone else. Now, maybe a hired killer might hesitate to kill a cop. Maybe not. I don't know. But one thing I do know is they will not think twice about offing some nosy private investigator. Trust me. I know what I'm talking about."

Tracy looked into his eyes and could feel the seriousness of his words.

"So, what, then, Jimmy? We just shrug and let it go?"

He frowned.

"Maybe," he said. "Sometimes that's for the best. You can't save the world, kid. We're born into a world of flames, and you can spend your whole life trying to put the fires out. But you'll just end up old and tired, and the flames will burn on long after you're dead. Now, it's a shame this girl got herself killed. But it sounds like she was playing in a busy street."

Tracy narrowed her eyes.

"So, she had it coming. Is that it?"

He sighed.

"It's not like that," he said. "I'd love for whoever killed her to face the justice they deserve. But I don't want you to end up just like her. Hell, I don't want to either."

Tracy raised her eyebrows.

"What? Are you afraid, Jimmy?"

He shrugged.

"It's good sense to know when to be afraid. It's kept me alive for this long. There's a time for reckless courage, and there's a time to be smart. You got balls, kid. But you can't let them lead you around. It doesn't make you strong. It makes you predictable."

Tracy shook her head.

"Even if what you're saying is true. Even if this angle is dangerous. I'm already in too deep. I took the senator's money. I need to show some progress."

Jimmy raised his eyebrows.

"And what if it all leads back to his people?" he said. "What if it isn't some clandestine operation by some billion-dollar special interest? What if it's the senator's people, and he just doesn't realize it? Even if it all went down without his knowledge, the blowback is going to be huge. The media will be all over it. He won't be happy. Even if you are able to solve this case somehow, I just don't see how things work out in your favor. There are so many ways it can go wrong. So, why sprint into a buzzsaw?"

Tracy swallowed and shook her head.

"If it goes wrong, it goes wrong," she said. "I'll face the consequences. But you don't have to. If you don't want to be a part of this, I'll give you your cut now, and we can part ways."

She looked into his face, but it was closed as ever. He was quiet for a while, and then he finally spoke.

"Nah," he said. "I'll see it through."

She offered a weak smile.

"Thanks, Jimmy."

He sighed and looked over at Tony.

"Don't thank me yet," he said. "We still gotta make this idiot dance to our tune."

They turned and looked at Tony, who watched them with his rat-like stare, the wheels turning in his ill-made mind, as he contemplated ways to flip things in his favor.

Chapter 12

Tracy stood in her apartment, a finger pulling the edge of a curtain as she peered out the window at the traffic several stories below. Even this late in the night, a steady stream of cars flowed through the neighborhood, some honking now and again at the occasional brazen pedestrian who lazily crossed the streets with an inebriated stagger and tired yawn.

She watched each one with a discerning eye, but all seemed to be legitimate drunks. Or if they were spies of some kind, for the senator or some private intelligence agency, she figured they were meant to be distractions from real spies—those skilled professionals lurking unseen like ghosts in the shadows.

A light popped on behind her, and Tracy spun around.

"Shut that off!" she hissed.

Tony tilted his head at her like a flummoxed dog.

"What's the big deal?"

She rushed over and shut off the lamp.

"The big deal is that people can see inside."

Tony shrugged.

"Anyone worth his salt would probably have some kind of night vision goggles, don't you think?"

She narrowed her eyes at him.

"Just sit down and shut up."

He put his hands up in surrender and plopped down on her sofa.

"You got anything to eat?" he asked. "I'm getting a little lightheaded."

She turned away without responding and walked back to the window. With a gentle tug, she pulled the edge of the curtain in time to see Jimmy casually crossing the street with his hands in his pockets, his head down as he shuffled along with the slightest limp. She watched as he entered her apartment building. Then, she scanned the streets with a discerning eye until she heard a knock at the door.

Tony jumped a little at the sound.

"Relax," she said as she crossed the room.

She unlocked the door and let Jimmy inside.

"Well?" she asked.

Jimmy glanced at Tony, who squirmed in his seat.

"We should hear something in the next couple hours."

Tracy nodded, and they both looked at Tony.

"You ready for this?" she asked.

He nodded.

"Sure. This is child's play for someone like me."

Tracy and Jimmy looked at each other.

"Here," said Jimmy as he pulled an old flip phone from his pocket. "This is an old-school burner phone. It's the phone number I included in the letter. Normally you'd dispose of it when you're done. But that's only if you don't want to be found."

They both looked at Tony again, and he swallowed the void in his throat.

"Alright," said Tracy as she took the phone. "Listen up, Tony. When that phone rings, you do it just like we rehearsed. No freelancing. You got it?"

Tony raised his eyebrows.

"Of course," he said.

Tracy and Jimmy looked at each other again.

"I need a drink," said Jimmy.

Tony perked up.

"Pour me one too."

Tracy pinned him with a glare.

"No," she said as she set the little phone on the coffee table.

He sunk back against the sofa and folded his arms.

Tracy followed Jimmy into the kitchen and watched while he collected a half-filled bottle of whiskey. He opened a cabinet and peered inside.

"You really need to do some dishes," he said as he plucked a coffee cup from inside.

She started to speak as he unscrewed the lid to the bottle. But her voice cut off at the sound of the ringing phone.

"Hey," said Tony from the other room. "I think it's them."

Jimmy and Tracy looked at each other and then rushed into the other room.

"Answer it," said Jimmy.

Tony looked at Tracy.

"Now?"

"Yes," said Tracy. "Hurry up. Put is on the speaker setting, so we can hear."

They watched as Tony stood straight and ran a hand over his slicked-back hair. He whispered a few words to himself, took a breath and shut his eyes.

Tracy and Jimmy looked at each other as the phone continued to ring.

"Godammit," said Jimmy.

"Tony!" said Tracy.

He opened his eyes and exhaled. Then, he calmly bent over and collected the phone from the table.

"Yeah," he said as he answered the call.

There was a pause.

"Start talking," said Tony. "I'm not in the mood for games."

Tracy and Jimmy exchanged looks, but Tony didn't seem to notice.

"This is Thomas Stone," said the caller. "I am the campaign manager for Senator Jenkins. We received your letter, and we're a little disturbed by it."

"Good," said Tony. "So, you know I mean business."

There was whispering on the other end of the line. Tony looked up at Tracy and raised his eyebrows. She turned toward Jimmy, but he only shrugged.

"Who's that you're talking to?" asked Tony at last.

"I'm sorry," said Thomas. "That was the senator's attorney, Andrew Stallings. He'll be monitoring this phone call, along with the senator's head of security, Emmerich Wagner."

Tony looked at Tracy, who shrugged.

"Whatever," said Tony. "But no cops."

"No," said Thomas. "No, of course not. We want to keep this as quiet as possible."

"I'll bet you do," said Tony.

He began pacing around the room, his face relaxing as he sank into his element.

"And can you tell me your name?" asked Thomas.

"Nah," said Tony. "Let's just hold off on that for now."

"Fine, then," said Thomas. "Can you tell me what you want?"

"Money," said Tony. "I want money. In return, you get my silence about the senator's little extramarital dalliance, as well as whatever hand he had in my friend's death."

It was quiet for a moment, followed by more whispering.

"I can assure you," said Thomas at last, "the senator had nothing to do with your friend's death."

"Sure," said Tony. "Whatever you say." There was more whispering, and Tony rubbed his jaw. "Are you the one in charge?" he asked at last. "If not, why don't you just put the others on the phone? I don't have time for bullshit. Let's cut to the chase, shall we?"

"Yes, of course," said Thomas. "Can you first tell me how you came to obtain your information?"

Tony looked at Tracy, who nodded.

"I thought the letter made it pretty plain," he said. "I was a friend of Dana Brockers. She confided in me. That good enough for you?"

There was more whispering.

"I'm losing my patience here," said Tony.

"Mr. Sullivan," said a harsh, raspy voice.

Tony's eyes widened as he looked at Tracy and Jimmy, who glanced at each other with obvious concern.

"Who is this?" asked Tony. "And how do you know my name?"

"I am the senator's head of security," hissed Emmerich. "It is my job to know things."

Tony looked at Tracy, and for a moment, his face seemed to falter. But then, as if by will, he regained his conman posture, and confidence seemed to radiate from his pores.

"Good for you," he said. "Why are you butting into my conversation?"

"I have questions of my own," said Emmerich. "Before I will allow this arrangement to take place, you will answer them. Is that clear?"

Tony shrugged.

"Or, I can just hang up this phone and call the media," he said. "And maybe the cops while I'm at it."

"No," said Emmerich. "I don't think you will do that."

"And why's that?" asked Tony.

"Because there's no money in that."

Tony frowned at Tracy and Jimmy, who were poised on the edges of their seats.

"Alright, smart guy," said Tony. "Ask your questions."

"Are you working on behalf of anyone?" asked Emmerich. "A private detective, perhaps?"

Tracy and Jimmy looked at each other. Tony gave a shrug.

"I work for me," he said. "Me, me, me, me."

"And yet," said Emmerich. "You were working with Dana Brockers."

Tony pulled the phone away from his face and held a hand over it.

"Who the fuck is this guy?" he asked Tracy.

"Just throw him off the scent," she whispered.

Tony pulled the phone back to his ear.

"Were you talking to someone?" asked Emmerich. "An accomplice, perhaps."

Jimmy leaned over to Tracy.

"This is going south," he whispered.

She pushed him away and watched as Tony placed a hand on his hip.

"Listen, here, you nosey fuck," he said. "It doesn't matter if I'm working alone or not. I could be conspiring with the entire roster of the god damn New York Yankees. The only thing that matters is keeping your guy's dirty laundry out of the news. Now, put the other guy back on the phone, so we can get down to business."

"You are very convincing," said Emmerich. "But I'm afraid no business will take place until I am fully satisfied."

Tony hung up the phone, and Tracy leaped to her feet.

"What are you doing?" she yelled.

He flinched and stumbled backward.

"Relax," he said. "This is all part of the dance."

141

She held her hands out to her side.

"Dance?" she asked. "What fucking dance?"

He shrugged.

"Trust me," he said. "I've been at this game a long time, and when they start trying to strongarm you, that's when you pull the ripcord to show you're serious."

Tracy looked at Jimmy, but he only shrugged.

"What if they don't call back?" asked Tracy.

Tony almost laughed.

"Oh, they'll call back."

She shook her head and looked at Jimmy.

"What about the questions?" she asked. "You think they're onto us?"

Jimmy frowned up at her.

"They might just be fishing," he said. "Or maybe he had another tail on you and saw the two of you together at some point."

"Shit," she said as she put a hand on her forehead.

The phone rang, and they all looked at each other.

"Yeah," said Tony as he answered the call.

"Mr. Sullivan, this is Thomas again. I apologize for the difficulties."

"Good," said Tony as he smiled at Tracy and Jimmy. "Don't let it happen again."

"Of course not," said Thomas. "We're prepared to do business."

Tony licked his lips and raised his eyebrows.

"Good," he said. "Let's talk money."

"Of course," said Thomas. "But first, have you told anyone else about this? That is, have you shared your knowledge about Senator Jenkins and Ms. Brockers with anyone else?"

Tony looked at Tracy, who shook her head, no.

"No," said Tony. "But it's right on the tip of my tongue, so let's start talking money."

"Yes," said Thomas. "We are prepared to give you the same deal we gave Ms. Brockers. That's $10,000 a month for your silence. Is that acceptable?"

Tony looked at Tracy, who shook her head, yes.

"Hold on a second," said Tony.

He pulled the phone away.

"What are you doing?" whispered Tracy. "Say, yes."

Tony's eyes traveled from Tracy to Jimmy. Then, he inhaled through his teeth.

"Here's the deal," he said. "I get to keep any money that comes through. Otherwise, this whole thing is over right now."

Tracy shook her head.

"No," she whispered. "That money could end up being evidence in a crime. No one keeps it."

"Are you there, Mr. Sullivan?" said Thomas.

Tony put the phone to his ear.

"Give me a second."

He lowered the phone and looked at Tracy, his eyes careful to avoid Jimmy's hateful glare.

"Sorry," he said to Tracy. "But I can't agree to that. I may be risking my life here. You know? I mean, you're basically using me as bait. So, either I get the money, or I tell them right now that you two put me up to this."

Tracy looked at Jimmy, who was shaking his head at the floor.

"God damn it," whispered Tracy. She looked up at Tony, who was watching her with smug satisfaction. "Fine. Just get it done."

He grinned.

"Mr. Sullivan?" said Thomas.

Tony put the phone to his ear.

"Sorry," he said. "Where were we?"

Thomas sighed.

"We are prepared to offer you $10,000, delivered monthly, the same arrangement we made with Ms. Brockers."

Tony looked up at the ceiling and sucked his cheek, as if sampling the flavor of some vague thought.

"Nah," he said. "Let's make it a couple million."

Tracy's jaw fell open as she frantically began waving her hands. But Tony had already turned his back and started walking to the other side of the room.

"Excuse me?" asked Thomas.

"You heard me," said Tony. "Two million dollars. A one-time payment. None of this installment bullshit. I'm a busy man. I don't have time for weekly meetings."

"Absolutely not," Emmerch hissed. "That's outrageous."

"Ah," Tony said. "The security guy. Still listening, are we?"

"Listen, here, you piece of shit," hissed Emmerich.

143

"No, you listen," said Tony. "I don't like you. So, put the other fellow back on the phone. Or I'm gonna hang up and start dialing the New York Times."

The line filled with frantic whispering, and Tony smiled. He turned to face Tracy and Jimmy, who were both standing, their hands balled into fists as they stared at him with murderous intent. Tony swallowed and turned back around.

"I'm losing my patience here," he said.

"Mr. Sullivan," said Thomas, "we may be able to offer you more than $10,000, but two million is an unreasonable sum. Now if we could just—"

Tony hung up the phone.

"What are you doing?" yelled Tracy.

Tony started to speak, but Jimmy had crossed the room and collected him by the collar.

"Whoa, whoa, whoa!" said Tony. "Take it easy. It's all under control."

"Under control?" said Tracy. "You just hung up on them again after asking for 200 times what they offered. You've blown this whole thing."

Tony licked his lips and looked up at Jimmy, who looked lost in a haze of psychopathic rage.

"Just relax," he said. "Both of you relax. It's better this way."

Tracy crossed the room and stood before the small man. She held her hands out to her side.

"How in the world is it better this way?"

He gave a nervous shrug.

"Think about it," he said. "If I'd agreed to ten grand a month, this thing might have run on for a year or more. This way, they'll make their move right off the bat. Whoever they are."

Tracy looked at Jimmy, who was pondering Tony's words. He dropped the man and stepped back.

"He's got a point," he said. "I hate to admit it, but it makes sense."

Tracy shook her head.

"Not if it's a one-time payment," she said. "He has to appear to be an ongoing thorn in the senator's side. Otherwise, why would the senator's staff or a third-party killer intervene?"

Jimmy nodded.

"Then, ask for monthly payments."

144

Tracy raised her eyebrows.

"Two million a month?" she said. "They will never agree to that. Assuming they even call back at all. This is a disaster."

Tony looked at each of them and raised his hands up.

"Listen, you two gotta calm down. This is how these things work. It's like a negotiation. First, you set them up and make them think you're unreasonable. You shoot big, and they freak out. Then, they try to bring you back to the middle. But what they don't know is that the middle is where you wanted to be the whole time."

Tracy looked at Jimmy, who shrugged.

"Just say the word, and I'll knock his teeth out," he said.

She approached Tony and took him by the ear.

"Jesus," he yelped, as she gave it a hard twist.

"Listen, you dumb fuck" said Tracy. "When they call back—if they call back—you tell them 100 thousand monthly. Alright? Not a penny more. Do you understand?"

He grimaced and nodded.

"Sure. Just let go of my fucking ear."

She released him, and he jerked back.

"Jesus," he said. "You two are cut from the same cloth."

The phone rang, and they all looked at it.

"Is it them?" asked Tracy.

"Of course, it's them," said Tony as he shook loose from Jimmy. "Now, just sit back and let me do my thing."

"Wait," said Tracy.

He looked at her while the phone rang.

"One hundred thousand monthly," she said. "Not a penny more. Do you understand?"

Tony raised his eyebrows.

"And I keep whatever comes through," he said. "Even if it takes a year."

Tracy looked at Jimmy, but he only shrugged. She looked back at Tony and nodded.

"Fine," she said. "Now, make the fucking deal."

Tony grinned and answered the phone.

"Yeah."

"Mr. Sullivan," said a new voice.

They all exchanged looks.

"Who's this?" asked Tony.

"This is Andrew Stallings. I am the senator's attorney. We are prepared to accept your terms. But you will need to sign a non-disclosure agreement in return."

Tony began pacing.

"I ain't signing shit," he said. "Anyway, I don't appreciate the way I've been treated. So, things have changed. It's gonna be 200 grand a month, every fucking month. Until I say otherwise."

Tracy put her hands on her head and looked at Jimmy, who was wearing an infuriating 'I told you so' expression.

"What?" asked Stallings.

"You heard me," said Tony. "Those are my final terms, and they're non-negotiable. You wanna argue? I add another 100 grand every time. You get me?"

The line was quiet except for the frantic whispering.

"Fine," said Stallings. "How do you want to handle the transactions?"

Tony looked at Tracy, who appeared as if she was about to spontaneously combust.

"We'll meet in two weeks," he said. "I gotta sort some things out. I'll call you with the details. Two weeks. Keep your phone handy."

With that, he hung up the phone.

"Holy shit!" he said as his face lit up. "Can you believe this shit?"

Jimmy looked at Tracy, and she gave a little nod. In an instant, he was across the room, his face darkening, fingers balled into big fleshy hammers. As if struggling to find traction on ice, Tony stumbled backward. And then he gasped as Jimmy drove a fist into his stomach. Tracy watched as the small man collapsed to the floor.

"What was that shit?" she asked. "We said 100 thousand. What the fuck is wrong with you?"

Tony braced his hands against the carpet and wheezed, his face red as a fire hydrant. Jimmy plucked him up from the carpet and dragged him across the apartment.

"Stay there," he said as he tossed him onto the sofa.

He approached Tracy, and the two moved to the dining area.

"Jesus Christ," said Tracy. "What a disaster."

"I don't know," said Jimmy. "To be honest, it went better than I expected."

She looked across the apartment at Tony, who was starting to get his breath back.

"This may be a huge mistake," she said.

Jimmy nodded.

"Maybe," he said. "But it's too late to turn back now. Anyway, we've got two weeks to get our ducks in a row. So, we'd better start covering all the bases."

Tracy nodded.

"What do we do with him?" she asked. "He'll bolt the first chance he gets."

Jimmy shook his head.

"Nah. He won't skip out on the chance for that kind of money. But he may try to screw us over. Probably in a way we can't even imagine."

Tracy glanced over at Tony, who had fully regained his composure and was now doing his best to keep his eyes off the two of them.

"How?" she asked.

Jimmy shrugged.

"I have no idea. But in my experience, a good con artist is always three steps ahead. They see angles that are invisible to normal people. I wouldn't even begin to consider all the ways he could fuck us over. We just need to keep him under wraps."

Tracy nodded.

"I'll keep an eye on him."

Jimmy shook his head.

"No. I'll keep him with me."

Tracy raised her eyebrows.

"He's no good to us dead."

Jimmy gave a soft chuckle.

"Don't worry," he said. "He may have a few extra bruises, but he'll live. In the meantime, you need to work on shedding your tail. If you have one, which I'm guessing is pretty likely."

She raised her eyebrows.

"I haven't noticed anyone following me. Not recently, at least."

Jimmy frowned.

"You never do, kid. Not when they know what they're doing."

Tracy looked at him doubtfully.

"I'll be careful."

He nodded.

"Good."

They both looked at Tony, who seemed fully recovered from Jimmy's punch, his attention now fixated on some dirt he was trying to pry from a fingernail.

"What if there is no attempt on his life?" Tracy asked. "What if the senator pays the money, and that's the end of it?"

Jimmy shrugged.

"Then, we get to do it all again next month. And I have the worst roommate in the history of roommates. But 200 grand is a big price. I'd wager we'll see something. Once word of this trickles through the grapevine, whoever killed Dana Brockers will want this whole thing tied up as soon as possible, especially when they start digging into Tony's background. They won't want to leave a loose end like him active for too long."

Tracy looked up at Jimmy.

"Why are you doing this?" she asked. "I mean, don't get me wrong, I'm going to make it worth your while. But why risk yourself for my shit storm?"

Jimmy looked over at Tony and then back at her.

"I don't know," he said. "Maybe I've grown fond of you." He shrugged. "Or maybe I just don't believe in you, and I think you'll fuck things up without some help."

She glared at him.

"Such a gentleman."

He looked offended.

"I am a gentleman."

"Really?" she asked.

"Absolutely," he said. "I'm such a gentleman, I always wait for the lady to suggest splitting the bill before I ever bring it up."

She shook her head, and they both looked at Tony, who seemed to have perfected the subtle art of ignoring their heated gazes.

"How's he going to fuck this up?" she asked.

Jimmy shook his head.

"I don't know. But he'll try."

148

Chapter 13

Jimmy had been right. There were people following Tracy. What's more, there appeared to be people following the people following her. And perhaps even people following them. People she couldn't see, like the ones Emmerich had described. Shadowy whispers of men moving with the stealth and agility of panthers, dipping in and out of shadows throughout the urban landscape.

The man with the mustache was no panther.

Impatient and easily bored, he fidgeted nervously as he lurked at the edge of every block, his foot tapping the pavement as he chain-smoked a new cigarette every 20 minutes.

Balding and overweight, he wore an ill-fitting blue polo shirt and a pair of aviator sunglasses. His whole getup screamed undercover cop, and Tracy decided that John had likely put him on her tail since their meeting after Dana's murder.

Despite his forced nonchalance, the man stood out like a sore thumb. And whenever Tracy glanced at him, he habitually held a finger to his lips and looked all around as if searching for an address, like a bad actor in some community theater play.

It took her no time to lose him. She simply dipped into a woman's lingerie store and plucked a spicy little number from the rack. This was a frilly garment that seemed to be made of shoestrings. And she held it high as she made her way across the store to the dressing rooms, where she casually discarded it before slipping out the back door and into the rear alley, while the mustached man paced around the front of the store, blushing like a teenage boy.

The second man was a bit harder. In fact, it took her a while to realize he existed at all. Plain-looking and unremarkable, he was easy to overlook if you weren't really looking. But Tracy was looking, and he eventually tipped his hand due to simple repetition.

Three times she'd seen him, each time at different locations. He might have been another one of Emmerich's men. Or, he could have just been another cop. Whatever the case, he was good but not great. And she lost him using one of her father's little strategies that essentially involved taking an elevator up a high rise, getting out midway, and then taking the stairs back down to the lobby.

It was all child's play until she started seeing ghosts. Driven by an increasing paranoia, she began to see suspicious people all around her. They seemed to be everywhere, scattered about the crowds, at least three or maybe four men and women, all perfectly normal, except for the subtlest movements that might have been nothing, or everything.

Amid the frantic buzz of taxis, honking horns and barking street vendors, a young man sat at a table drinking coffee outside a cafe. About 100 feet from him, a middle-aged woman read a magazine alone atop a park bench, her brows pinched as she concentrated on the text. Across the busy street, an old man walked a leashed dog, who sniffed a tree and pawed at the ground. And while the rush of people flowed about them, all three seemed to intermittently hold fingers to their ears, as if straining to listen for a handful of seconds before returning to their activities without ever looking her way.

Tracy looked up at the rooftops and thought she saw someone move away from the edge of a restaurant. She blinked and looked again. She rubbed her eyes and shook her head as if to jostle the paranoia out of her brain.

She glanced around and assessed the entire area with a fresh perspective. But now, everyone seemed suspicious. The woman on the bench, the old man, the dog itself. Even a child seemed to be watching her with a pair of narrow eyes as he licked an ice cream cone that bent precariously to one side. She glared back at him and put a hand on her hip just as her phone buzzed in her pocket.

"Yeah," she said as she put it to her ear.

"What are you doing?" asked Jimmy. "It'll be dark soon."

"What am I doing?" she asked. "I'm doing what you told me to do. I'm getting out in public trying to flush out my tails."

"And?" he asked.

She looked at the young boy, who was now mourning the loss of his ice cream, which had toppled over into the ground.

"I think I may be crazy."

Jimmy chuckled.

"Don't sweat it," he said. "You ain't the first to see ghosts. Everyone gets paranoid if they spend enough time in this business."

She glanced at the other suspicious faces, who all seemed a bit too casual.

"I don't know," she said. "I definitely had a couple of shadows. But they were pretty obvious and easy to shake. Something tells me there's more, but I can't be sure."

"Well," said Jimmy. "You need to shake them before tonight, or you will lead them right to the meet-up."

She looked all around, but no one returned her stare.

"Any suggestions?"

It was quiet for a moment.

"Just get on a subway train and then jump out the door as it gets going."

"That's it?" she asked. "I thought you'd have something a little less cliché."

"Clichés become clichés because they work. Anyway, you might have to do it twice, especially if you really do have professionals on your tail. Then again, you may just be getting paranoid. It may all just be in your head."

She looked around and sighed.

"You're always such a calming presence in my life, Jimmy."

"Sorry, kid. I don't know what to tell you. But you do need to hurry up and get here before I kill Tony and blow this whole deal. He won't shut the fuck up, and I'm running out of patience."

She hung up the phone and made her way up the street to the subway entrance, which vomited out a stream of people who pushed past her as she made her way down the stairs. Doing her best to remain nonchalant, she paid her fare at the ticket machine without looking around. Then, she passed through the turnstile before joining a small crowd gathering at the subway platform. There she waited, her eyes peering into the dark tunnel in wait for the train, as her mind resisted the urge to look back for the middle-aged woman, the old man, or anyone else who might be on her heels.

151

As she settled among the other commuters, she did her best to blend in. Someone in the small mass of people had what could only be described as aggressive body odor, and the smell mingled with the acrid scent of metal, intensifying her unease.

The distant rumble of approaching trains echoed through the tunnel, drowning out the low chatter of the people around her. Below her feet, the faint flickering of the overhead fluorescent lights revealed small patches of grime, and dirt and what she hoped was just a different color of dirt all throughout the worn tiles.

At last, the train arrived with a piercing screech of metal on metal. Tracy stepped aside as people flowed out onto the platform. Then, she followed the crowd into the train and stood just inside the door. She watched and waited as people found their seats. Then, when the platform had emptied, she quickly stepped back outside only to find that someone had mirrored her movements one exit down.

It was the middle-aged woman from before, and she stood just outside the subway, her eyes locked with Tracy, face expressionless and cold. They stood and stared at each other, while Tracy's heart thundered in her chest. Then, just as the doors began to close, Tracy stepped back inside the train, a few strands of hair catching as she slipped through like smoke.

In a panic, the woman turned and tried to mimic her movements. But the door had already closed. As she cursed mutely outside the window, the woman walked alongside the train while it crawled forward, her eyes watching Tracy through the glass as she disappeared into the tunnel.

Hours later, Tracy stood next to Jimmy at a small, dimly lit bar on the south side of town. Across the street, there was a little diner with a sign that flickered intermittently with sickly bursts of red neon light. Tracy eyed it through the window and then turned back toward Tony, who was chewing his nails as he squirmed amid a small booth. She watched him for a moment and then looked past Jimmy at the dimly lit surroundings, where rough-looking men loomed featureless in small booths tucked away amid the shadows.

The place smelled of tobacco and old moldy beer mats, and the customers looked like the type of people who might rape you if given the chance. Tracy shuddered on the inside and shook her head at Jimmy.

"Quite a place you've picked out."

He shrugged.

"We don't want cops interfering. They don't patrol around here. At least for the most part."

She sighed and looked at Tony, who had chewed past his fingernails and into the flesh of his thumbs.

"Take a deep breath," she said.

He looked up at her.

"It's nothing. I'm always like this before a con. It's just adrenaline. Once things get started, I'm as cool as the other side of the pillow."

Tracy and Jimmy exchanged looks.

"Alright," said Tracy. "Let's run through it again."

She sat at the other side of the booth and looked at him.

"Just go across the street and grab a seat at the diner. Then, you just wait. At some point, the senator's campaign manager will bring you the money. Take it, but try not to say anything. No more of this bullshit freelancing. Keep it short and simple."

Tony nodded.

"Sure."

Tracy glared at him.

"I mean it, Tony."

He held up a hand.

"Relax," he said. "You got nothing to worry about."

Tracy and Jimmy exchanged looks.

"Listen," said Tracy. "Once you have the money, you need to stall for a little while. Go use the bathroom. Give the senator's campaign manager time to leave. Then, come outside and walk up the block just like we talked about. Head down the alley on 14th. Jimmy will be hiding there. If someone follows you, he'll be there waiting."

Tony scratched his jaw.

"What if this killer, whoever it is, what if they rush me on the street?"

Tracy shook her head.

"That's not their way," she said. "They won't want to bring attention with a gunshot. They work with knives. Anyway, I'll be close

153

by. If someone makes a move before you get to the alley, I'll intervene. I promise."

He looked up at her with an uncertain expression.

"And what if no one shows up?" he asked.

She shrugged.

"Then, we do the whole thing again at the next payment."

He nodded.

"Well, shit," he said. "What's the point of life without taking a risk or two? Am I right?"

Jimmy put a hand on his shoulder.

"Don't fuck this up, and your legs will remain unbroken."

Tony looked up at him and swallowed.

"Sure."

Jimmy gave a little squeeze. Then, he released him and walked away.

"I don't think he likes me very much," said Tony as he rubbed his shoulder.

"Don't worry about it," said Tracy. "Are you ready?"

He looked at her and shrugged.

"Sure."

She nodded.

"Alright," she said. "We'll be watching. Go on, now."

She watched as Tony stood and walked out of the bar. When he was gone, Jimmy approached, and they both looked out the window, their eyes sweeping the area as Tony hurried across the desolate street, his small body a dark silhouette as it moved through the weak splotches of amber-hued streetlights. .

"How's he going to fuck this up?" asked Tracy.

Jimmy shook his head.

"I don't know."

They watched as he went inside the diner and claimed a table. Through the big exterior window, they could see only a portion of his body, as he ordered a coffee from the waitress.

"How long?" asked Tracy.

Jimmy checked his watch.

"About thirty minutes."

They sat in silence, their eyes peering through the window glass, sweeping left to right as they assessed every hobbling vagrant and the occasional passing car. At one point, a server approached, and

154

Jimmy ordered a beer. He sipped it and sat back in his seat, while Tracy's eyes bored into the exterior night.

"You'll dull your senses," she said without looking at him.

Jimmy looked down at his beer and shrugged.

"They were never that sharp to begin with."

Tracy looked at him.

"We don't need Tony's throat getting slit open because you were too busy taking a piss."

He frowned at her and then looked at his beer.

"You got a point."

He pushed the beer away and checked his watch.

"Ten minutes late," he said.

Tracy stared across the street into the diner window, where Tony was tapping his shoe.

"Maybe they won't show."

Jimmy said nothing, his eyes squinting as he peered through the window. They sat quietly for a while amid the clinking glasses and clattering billiard balls. Someone at the bar yelled at the television. A woman erupted in drunken laughter behind them.

"There," said Tracy.

Jimmy leaned forward and squinted.

"I see him."

Out of the shadows came a slim, tall man, his head down, a satchel in one hand. He moved through the area like someone who'd rather be anywhere else, his body tense as he hurried toward the diner amid the gusty wind.

"That's Thomas," said Tracy.

Jimmy nodded, and they watched as he crossed the street and entered the diner. Inside, he immediately approached Tony, and the two shook hands. Then, he sat across from him and set the satchel on the table.

"We're in business," said Jimmy. "You are now an accomplice to criminal extortion."

Tracy ignored him and stared through the window. Inside the diner, the two men seemed to converse in a cordial manner. Then, after a few more minutes, Thomas stood and walked out the door. Tracy watched as he paused outside the diner and looked around. Then, she ducked down a little as his eyes moved toward the bar.

"Take it easy," said Jimmy. "He can't see in here."

"What if he comes inside?" she asked.

155

Jimmy frowned thoughtfully as he considered her words. But the senator's campaign manager wasn't the type to dip into seedy bars after midnight. And just as expected, he quickly walked away from the diner and disappeared the way he came.

"Alright," said Tracy. "Now, we wait."

They both looked across the street toward the diner. Inside, Tony was finishing up his coffee. He sipped slowly, almost lovingly, from the cup as if he had all the time in the world. Then, just as he had been instructed, he stood up and walked to the bathroom.

"Time for you to go," said Tracy.

Jimmy nodded and stood up. He turned to go and then stopped short. Tracy furrowed her brows as he turned back around.

"What is it?" she asked.

He looked at her and frowned.

"Spit it out, Jimmy," she said.

He looked at her and cleared his throat.

"Listen to me," he said. "If things go south, I recommend that you walk away."

She narrowed her eyes.

"What?"

He shrugged.

"If this blows up. If something goes wrong. Just walk away. Don't look back. Just turn around and disappear."

She shook her head.

"What are you talking about?"

He stared down at her, his eyes hard.

"I meant what I said before, Tracy. This is a criminal act. It's extortion of a U.S. senator with a lot of money involved. And if it ends with someone dead, you could end up facing some serious hard time in prison. We both could."

She shook her head.

"You're being ridiculous. The senator hired me to find the killer and clear his name. I have some leeway here. Anyway, the only way that would happen is if he pressed charges. And he's not going to do that if it means his name gets dragged through the mud."

Jimmy frowned at her.

"Or," he said. "Maybe he and his people deny ever hiring you in the first place. And you end up being the one investigated. For extortion. Who knows? Maybe for murder too."

Tracy stood up and held her hands out.

"Jesus Christ, Jimmy. You're just mentioning this now?"

He shrugged.

"I just thought of it now."

She rubbed her eye and shook her head.

"Just go wait in the alley," she said. "We don't have time for this right now."

He nodded.

"Just remember what I said."

With that, he turned and left the bar. Tracy watched through the window as he moved through the streets, his big body a featureless silhouette as he passed through the weak splotches of light from the dim streetlamps.

She sat back down and looked across the street toward the empty booth in the diner. She checked the time and waited, her eyes narrowing as she scanned the area. Minutes ticked away, but no one passed into her vision. Inside the diner, the booth sat empty. No sign of Tony. No sign of any customers at all. Tracy furrowed her brow and chewed her teeth. She checked the time and stood up. Then, she took a deep breath and sat back down.

More time passed, but Tony did not reappear. And after a while, she removed her phone and texted Jimmy.

"He's still in the bathroom."

She waited.

"Jimmy?"

A few more seconds passed.

"Just wait," he texted back.

She looked back across the street to the empty booth and then frowned down at her phone.

"He's 15 minutes late," she typed.

"You have to wait," he replied. "If you're seen, it blows the whole deal."

She looked back across the street into the diner, where a waitress had approached Tony's table and started wiping it down. Tracy bent over her phone and started typing.

"What if someone was in the bathroom already?" she typed. "What if he's in there with his throat cut?"

She stared at her phone and waited. Seconds passed, and then she got his reply.

"Go check it out."

She jumped to her feet and moved toward the door. Outside, it smelled like rain, but there were only a few low clouds blotting away the edges of a star-speckled sky. She lingered in the entryway a moment and looked around. The street was empty, save for a vagrant who shuffled aimlessly at the mouth of a distant alley. Tracy eyed him for a moment and then hurried across the road. The wind kicked up as she moved toward the diner, and she narrowed her eyes against flecks of dirt and debris that swirled up around her.

The diner door announced her presence with a sharp ding, and a waitress looked up with a tired yawn.

"Hello," said the young woman.

Tracy gave a nod and looked at the booth Tony had been sitting in. Then, she hurried toward the restrooms, while the waitress eyed her with an uncertain expression. When she reached the men's room door, she curled a fist and gave a hard knock.

"Tony."

She waited, but there was no response. Without hesitating, she opened the door and stepped inside. There was a urinal and a single stall, both in need of a good cleaning, and each unoccupied by Tony or anyone else. Tracy's heart throbbed in her chest.

She turned and rushed back to the waitress, who flinched a little at whatever she saw in Tracy's eyes.

"There was a man sitting here earlier," said Tracy. "Do you know where he went?"

The waitress shrugged.

"The bathroom, I guess."

Tracy turned and put a hand to her head. She withdrew her phone and started to type. Then, she paused and looked back at the kitchen. While the waitress protested, Tracy stormed around the counter and pushed her way through a pair of swinging metal doors. Steam from a hissing griddle warmed her face as she approached a sweaty middle-aged man in a soiled white t-shirt. He turned and regarded her with a frown, as she stared up into his pockmarked face.

"Where is he?" she asked.

The man gave her a puzzled look."

"Who?"

Tracy removed her pistol and leveled it at the man's face. The waitress yelped as she entered the kitchen, but Tracy paid her no mind.

"Where the fuck is the man from the bathroom?"

The cook's facade broke like cheap plastic, and he pointed a finger toward the back of the kitchen.

"He went out the back alley," he said. "He gave me a thousand dollars to keep quiet."

Tracy lowered her gun and ran toward the back of the kitchen. She put a hand on the doorknob and gave it a twist. She pushed, but the door only gave an inch. She threw a shoulder against it, straining with her body, but something was blocking it. She turned toward the cook, and he threw his hands up.

"Help me open it!" she said.

The man rushed over and gave the door a push, his teeth flashing white as he strained his aging muscles. At last, he stopped and backed away.

"I can't," he said as he pointed toward the crack of the door. "He must have rolled a dumpster in front of it. You'll have to go around the building."

Tracy turned and ran through the kitchen, while the cook and waitress looked at each other with befuddled expressions. A drunk couple was leaving the bar across the street as Tracy burst out of the diner. They stopped and watched as she frantically withdrew her phone and started sprinting up the block.

"What are you doing?" Jimmy whispered after two rings. "I'm standing here in a dark, quiet alley. You're gonna give my position away."

"He's gone," she said.

"What?"

"The little fucker is gone," she said. "He slipped out the back alley of the diner and blocked the door with a dumpster. We're screwed."

It was quiet for a moment.

"Jimmy!"

"I'm here," he said. "Motherfucker."

"I'm going after him," said Tracy. "But I have to go all the way around the block. I need you to try to cut him off if you can."

It was quiet for a few seconds more.

"Jimmy! God dammit."

"I'm here," he said with a sigh. "Alright. I'm on it. But listen for a second—"

"We don't have time!" she said. "Just go now!"

"Wait," said Jimmy. "Just listen. You need to be careful, ok? Don't hurry so fast you get sloppy. That little rat is more dangerous than he looks. I can promise you. And he's desperate now too. I wouldn't put anything past him. He might hide in the shadows somewhere and gut you with a knife if it means getting away with that money and avoiding my fist in his face."

"Just hurry," said Tracy as she ended the call.

She rounded the edge of the building and withdrew her pistol as she stood at the mouth of a long, dark alley. Without hesitating, she ran into the dark passage, which seemed to swallow her up like a great hungry mouth. The clicks of her shoes detonated in the quiet as she raced forward, her gun up and sweeping all around. As she pushed deeper into the alley, the light from the street behind her faded to near-nothing. And the path before her turned almost entirely black, save for the faint moonlight, which cast the soiled stretch of narrow pavement in a very dim, almost blue glow.

She paused to catch her breath. On either side of her, a pair of tall buildings flanked the pathway, encasing the dim-lit vein that threaded through the city.

When her eyes had calibrated to the low light, she stepped cautiously among the piles of discarded trash and debris, her gun up and darting about in search of the subtlest movements.

With every creeping footstep, the shadowed recesses of doorways and dumpsters offered endless places to hide. She regarded each with suspicious intensity, her fingers flexing around her pistol as she moved through the labyrinth of brick and asphalt, where rickety fire escapes clung to buildings like great insects, caked in rust.

All around her, the foul air seemed charged by the eerie silver glow of moonlight, impenetrable shadows seeming to lunge outward and grasp at her ankles as she crept into the stinking gloom.

Slowly and carefully, she moved forward, her eyes scanning efficiently, every sense alert and alive. As she watched the shadows for movement, her chest swelled with rapid breaths, the air thick with the smell of damp decay, fingers choked white as she strangled her pistol grip.

As she crept, shadowed movements summoned her gun and her eyes. A stray cat, a drug-addled vagrant. Rats of phenomenal size. With each clattering noise, she spun and pointed her gun, her squinting eyes struggling to cut through the darkness.

She moved forward, her shoes echoing softly against the pavement as she threw open a dumpster and looked inside. Then, having cleared it, she looked around and moved on to the next shadowed alcove, where she found only more rats and dumpster filth.

Onward she moved, faster now, each creeping stride a test of nerve amidst the shadowed doorways and reeking receptacles. With every creeping step, her sharp eyes dissected the brick and asphalt maze. And still, she pressed deeper into the gloom, probing the alley for hidden dangers until she reached the other side of the block. Then she knelt behind a weathered brick wall and lowered her pistol. As she massaged the burn in her tired shoulder, her eyes peered into the low light, probing for flashes of movement.

And then, amid the intermittent gusts of wind, she heard the distinct sound of footsteps around the corner. Slowly and quietly, she stood up straight and pressed against the wall, her heart throbbing as the footsteps grew louder.

Someone was coming toward her up another intersecting alley, their pace hurried and deliberate, shoe steps echoing softly against the broken pavement.

She took in several breaths and held her pistol against her chest. Then, with a sudden turn, she spun out from the alley and leveled her weapon.

Jimmy started and raised a hand.

"Easy," he said.

Tracy lowered her gun and looked at him.

"Anything?"

He shook his head.

"Fuck," hissed Tracy. "He got away!"

Jimmy frowned down at her.

"I circled the entire block," he said. "I cut him off. You should have flushed him right to me. So, either you walked right past him, or he still has to be around here somewhere."

They both looked to their left, where another very narrow alley shot off into the darkness between two dilapidated buildings. Tracy turned toward Jimmy, who nodded.

"Let's go," she said.

Jimmy paused for a moment and removed a small flashlight from his coat pocket. He flipped it on and illuminated the narrow path where it burrowed into the darkness.

"Watch our backs," he said as he led the way.

Tracy gave a thorough look behind them as the slender alleyway swallowed them whole. Slowly, they crept, Jimmy shining his flashlight around, illuminating the graffiti-laden walls. The narrow, claustrophobic alley was lined with fire escapes and rusty pipes, and they dipped their shoulders to keep from snagging on the old, oxidized protrusions.

As they neared the halfway point, Tracy hooked a hand around Jimmy's arm. He turned and looked back to see her gesturing toward one of the fire escape ladders, which loomed several feet above their heads.

"What if he went up?" she asked.

Jimmy looked at the ladder.

"How would he reach it?" he asked.

She shrugged.

"Maybe he stood on a dumpster and then pulled the ladder back up behind him."

Jimmy shook his head.

"Even he's not crazy enough to climb one of these antiques. That metal is 90 percent rust. It would crumble to dust in your hands. And that's if the bolts don't slip out of the mortar."

She nodded, and they moved on, while the wind howled around them, and rats skittered past their shoes,

At last, they emerged from the shadowy passage into a tiny, rectangular clearing. Tracy caught up and stood beside Jimmy. The alley had spilled out into a small moonlit courtyard, carpeted by a patch of untamed, overgrown vegetation that had sprung up between two neglected buildings.

Centered amid the little patch of ground, the remnants of a long-forgotten playground loomed ominously in the moonlight, a set of rusty swings creaking as they swung in the breeze.

"Wait," said Tracy. "Listen."

Jimmy strained to hear over the high squeal of the swings and the low whir of rushing wind. He shook his head and glanced back at her.

"What is it?" he asked.

Tracy shushed him and stepped forward, her gun up and pointed toward the shadows on the other side of the courtyard.

Jimmy followed her gaze and narrowed his eyes.

"What is it?"

"Shine the light," said Tracy as she took another step.

Jimmy raised the flashlight just in time to see a leg disappear around the corner into another narrow alley.

"Wait!" Jimmy yelled, but Tracy was already halfway across the courtyard.

He hurried after her, the flashlight bouncing with every step as he watched her disappear into the alley.

One of the swings swayed before him, and he shoved it aside as he sprinted toward the thin mouth of the unlit passage. Without hesitating, he barreled between the buildings into the pitch-dark gap, where he found Tracy standing alone amid the black.

"Where is he?" he asked as he struggled to catch his breath.

Tracy stood quietly, her eyes squinting down at the ground. Jimmy followed her gaze and lit the alleyway floor with his flashlight.

There lay Tony amid a growing puddle of blood, his throat gashed open, vacant eyes studying the moonlit sky.

The wind whined and whirred as it funneled through the alley, and somewhere within the noise, the faint sound of scuffling summoned Tracy's attention.

"There!" she said as she stabbed a finger toward the distant shadows.

Jimmy raised his flashlight and illuminated the other side of the alley, where a dark figure stood among the dumpsters, his face concealed within a black wool ski mask.

"Stop!" yelled Tracy as she raised her gun.

Without hesitating, the man turned away and leaped onto a dumpster. Amid the spotlight of Jimmy's flashlight, he seized one of the fire escape ladders, and it came down with a hesitant shriek, rust flakes pollinating the air as he started to climb.

"Shit," hissed Tracy as she hurried after him.

Jimmy took a couple of steps forward, his light tracking the man as he scaled the rickety metal like a great spider. Then, he lowered the light to see Tracy atop the dumpster.

"Wait!" he said.

But she already had a hand on the ladder.

"Tracy!" he yelled as she scrambled upward, her hands and feet nimbly at work while she climbed from ladder to balcony to ladder to balcony, up and up on the heels of the masked man.

Jimmy lowered his gun and watched as the two climbed higher and higher, Tracy's shoes clanging audibly against the metal rungs as she ascended into the rising black.

Now, the wind came harder as she pursued the figure through the vertical course of fire escapes and balconies, the night's harsh breath whipping past their faces as the ground fell away beneath them.

As they ascended the metal rungs, their shoes gave off sharp pings, which echoed in the night, while the faint sound of police sirens rang in the distance.

Old and ill-kept, the metal ladders jangled and jostled under Tracy's weight, and she felt her stomach flip as they rattled in their frames.

Up and up, they climbed, Tracy's pulse quickening as the world diminished in size beneath her feet.

High away, the man scaled rungs with reckless speed, occasionally pausing for brief moments to catch his breath. Tracy watched him while she climbed, her lungs burning as she forced herself upward against gravity's endless pull, against the screaming voices in her head.

Three stories above her, the man paused to rest. While he sucked the windy air, he watched her from a small balcony, a thin black silhouette in the dimly lit night. As if confused by her relentless pursuit, he tilted his head as he regarded her, and this made him look strangely alien to her squinting eyes.

Tracy's gritted teeth flashed white as she climbed toward him, hand over hand, sharp metallic pings exploding in the night as she hurried her pace.

All the while, the man watched her, his chest heaving as he gulped the warm night air. And then, he removed something from his pocket and leaned to the edge of the balcony, which hung from the building like a small metal cage.

Tracy pulled herself tight against the ladder as he raised his arm and hurled something downward. A flash of fire erupted in her arm as something struck her shoulder. She gasped and lost her grip, her left hand weakened by the blow and fumbling for a firm hold as gravity tugged her downward.

Flakes of orange rust broke loose beneath her footing, and she slipped from her perch. With a thin cry, she caught one of the rungs and squeezed it with all her might, while both legs dangled above the hard, distant ground.

Strangling the rungs with a desperate grip, she regained her footing and made her way up the decaying ladder, flinging her exhausted body onto the next balcony.

The man watched her for a moment longer, and then he turned and ascended the next ladder.

Excruciating pain moved like electricity through the left side of Tracy's body, as she lay on her back sucking in breath. With a trembling hand, she felt for her shoulder and grasped the handle of a knife. It was a decent-sized blade, but it had only punctured the skin before striking bone, and the wound bled like a boiling well when she plucked the knife free.

She tossed it aside and climbed to her feet. With a grimace, she approached the edge of the balcony and looked down. Far below, the dim glow of streetlights barely pierced the inky night, casting long, dizzying shadows that played tricks on her eyes.

She turned and looked upward. High above, the man had gained considerable distance in the vertical chase.

Cursing, Tracy removed her pistol and leaned back against the rusted rim of the balcony. Arching her spine, she pushed outward against the brittle metal, her mind struggling to ignore the groaning rail and the dark distance beneath her.

Narrowing her eyes, she aimed her gun and pulled the trigger. Sparks illuminated the darkness, and the man embraced the ladder as bullets tapped the brick around him.

Without hesitating, Tracy holstered the weapon and hurried up the next ladder, a little shriek escaping her lips as pain spidered through her arm.

The man looked down and saw her racing upward. Shaking his head, he picked up his pace in response, ascending higher and higher up the side of the building.

Tracy climbed faster, while the wind howled around her, threatening to snatch her from the ladder, which groaned and whined against her shifting weight.

Her pulse raced as she moved quicker and quicker, throwing caution to the wind as she scrambled ladder after ladder to close the gap.

Far below, the ground beckoned, an unforgiving expanse of concrete waiting to claim her with a single misstep.

With each rung conquered, the fear of falling gnawed at Tracy's resolve, her heart thudding in her chest, breaths shallow as she sipped the air through clenched teeth.

Suddenly, one of Tracy's hands missed its mark and slipped away as she tried to grasp the next rung. She felt her chin crash against metal as she grappled for a secure hold.

Her head swam, and the world spun, blood filling her mouth as her feet lost their hold on the ladder. In a mad panic, she lunged blindly, hooking one of the rungs with a single outstretched hand. The ladder shuddered and groaned as her falling body jerked it away from the building. The rusty bolts jiggled in their worn brick sockets and then fell still as she dangled above the city.

Tracy pinched her eyes shut and tried to steady the spinning world, as the weight of her entire body dangled beneath two curled fingers that clung to a single rung like a trembling claw.

The ladder groaned again, and panic flooded her veins like ice water, her stomach lurching as gravity tugged at her ankles.

By a feat of desperation or sheer will, she managed to clear the ringing in her head. Then, just as her fingers began to lose the last of their strength, she embraced the ladder and clung tight, while the whipping wind licked at her bruised and battered jaw.

She looked up and squinted into the high away night. The man's figure grew smaller as he climbed, disappearing and reappearing in the intermittent darkness.

Tracy shook away the cobwebs, her chin and shoulder aching, tongue gashed and bleeding where her teeth had punctured the flesh. She leaned over and spat the iron from her mouth. Then, she wrapped a hand around one of the rungs and forced herself up the ladder.

Nerves raw with adrenaline, she climbed, hand over hand, eyes fixated on the man, who had begun to tire as he neared the top of the building.

As he paused to catch his breath, Tracy climbed faster, her body fueled by an internal furnace of rage and fear.

Soon, she had closed the vertical gap, and when he saw her advancing upward, the man scrambled onto the next ladder and climbed toward the structure's precipice.

Tracy watched as he scaled the last few ladders. Then, he paused on a balcony and looked down, wide eyes narrowing as he watched her approach with white gritted teeth.

Chest burning, she forced one hand over the next, even as a rusty rung bent beneath her feet, even as her panicked mind screamed catastrophic thoughts into her ear.

When she was within two ladders, the man turned and drove a boot into a window. Glass exploded, and Tracy watched as the man forced his way inside like some parasitic creature pushing into an open wound.

A woman's scream split the night as he entered, and Tracy hurried up the final few ladders until she was up and onto the balcony.

Staggering on trembling knees, she withdrew her pistol, chest heaving as she struggled to catch her breath.

Another scream howled from within the interior of the building, and Tracy slipped through the opening, her gun up and darting about a small, lightless bedroom.

She breathed and hurried toward the open bedroom door, her training and instincts taking over for her dizzy, fatigued mind.

She crept out into a hallway, and there she saw the source of the screaming.

"Let her go," said Tracy as she took a step forward.

At the end of the hall, the man watched her from behind a middle-aged woman in a nightgown, his bright eyes narrowing as he held her like a human shield.

He had a second knife, and he held it to her throat. The woman looked at Tracy through wide, terrified eyes that leaked tiny rivers as the man pulled her backward to guard his slow retreat.

"I mean it," said Tracy as she took another step to keep pace.

The man continued to back up, the point of his blade bending the woman's neck flesh inward, as he watched Tracy without responding.

Then, having reached the end of the hall, he flung the sobbing woman toward Tracy and vanished around the corner.

The woman let out another scream as she collided with Tracy, who raised her gun and braced against the impact. As the woman collapsed to the floor, Tracy slipped around her and rushed down the hallway.

She turned the corner to see that the front door of the apartment was hanging open. Without hesitating, she sprinted across the room and spilled out into a dimly lit hallway.

She looked left and then right, where she saw the man fleeing, his knife glinting in the low light as he rounded the corner.

Tracy ran, her tired legs carrying her by sheer will as she panted the air.

When she reached the end of the hall, she paused for a moment and caught her breath before turning the corner with her gun up.

"Stop!" she yelled as she flexed her hand around the pistol grip.

The fleeing man had already run the length of the next hallway and was now frantically jabbing the button next to an elevator door.

Tracy leveled the pistol at the man's back and felt her finger curl around the trigger.

"Stop!"

A soft tone chimed as the light above the elevator illuminated. Tracy cursed and lowered the weapon, as her mind conjured thoughts of an errant shot searing through the doors and into some innocent tenant within the elevator.

As if sensing her reticence, the man relaxed and turned to face her just as the elevator doors split open.

"Stop!" yelled Tracy as she scrambled up the hallway.

The man regarded her with one last look, and then he turned toward the open elevator, where his face met Jimmy's fist.

As if his very soul had been plucked from his body, the man's knees buckled, and he collapsed backward onto the floor.

Tracy slowed and watched as Jimmy stepped off the elevator. He looked at her and shook out his hand. He flexed his fingers and assessed his knuckles, where the man's tooth had sliced into his skin.

"Shit," he said. "That's a tetanus shot."

Tracy approached and stood over the man, who lay gasping, his lips a mangled ruin as he choked and gagged on blood. He still held the knife loosely in his hand, and Tracy stood on his wrist until he let it clatter onto the floor. Then, she kicked it away and stared down at his face.

Jimmy rubbed his hand and looked at her.

"You're not gonna last in this business with this ready-fire-aim shit, kid."

She ignored him and crouched next to the man. While he blinked up at her, she gathered up the bottom of his ski mask and stripped it upward.

"I'll be damned," said Jimmy.

Tracy shook her head as she looked down at Thomas, who choked and coughed as he turned his gaze away.

"I suppose you're going to tell me this is all just you," she said. "And the senator had nothing to do with it."

He looked up at her.

"Lawyer," he whispered.

She shook her head at him and stood up.

"No man is this important," she said as she looked down at him.

Thomas stared up at her and raised his eyebrows, his mouth opening to show his red-stained teeth.

"He is."

Tracy looked at Jimmy, and they both shook their heads. Then, they gathered Thomas from the floor and waited for the cops to arrive.

Chapter 14

"Live from the heart of our city, this is KWYT Radio News, your number one source for local, national, and global news. Good evening. I'm Sandra Green.

"In a landmark ruling that has shocked the law enforcement community, highly decorated Homicide Detective Bradley Myers has been found guilty on six criminal counts associated with his handling of numerous murder cases.

"The jury, after hours of deliberation, convicted Myers earlier today on charges of tampering with evidence, false reporting, perjury, obstruction of justice, conspiracy, and misconduct in public office.

"This verdict comes at the end of a grueling six-week trial, during which Myers' 20-year career was meticulously scrutinized. Prosecutors presented a staggering volume of evidence, highlighting a pattern of corruption and malfeasance that, they argued, had undermined numerous criminal investigations.

"Now, as the dust settles, the local community grapples with the unsettling reality that a man sworn to uphold the law has instead been found to have repeatedly and intentionally violated it.

"As for Bradley Myers, he now faces a daunting future. Each of the six charges carries a sentence ranging from 5 to 20 years in prison. Sentencing will be held in two weeks, and we can expect a heavy hand from the judge, given the gravity of the charges and the betrayal of public trust.

"We'll continue to keep you updated on this story and all its implications. You're tuned in to WXYZ Radio News, where you can count on us to bring you the news you need to know. Coming up next, a statement from Senator Paul Jenkins regarding the disturbing recent incident associated with his campaign."

The news woman's voice faded to a low whisper as Tracy turned down the radio. She took a deep breath and sat back in her seat, her eyes watching the far end of the parking lot where Jimmy was approaching in the gloomy darkness.

As he limped closer, she thought about Bradley and tried to conjure feelings of satisfaction about his fate. About the apparent justice she'd help create. But it all seemed small and fruitless now for reasons she couldn't quite understand.

The passenger door opened, and Jimmy sat down beside her. He started to speak, but she silenced him with a finger.

"Hold on," she said. "Jenkins is giving a statement."

He shut the door, and they sat and listened, their faces frowning at the radio as Tracy turned up the volume.

"…and we're expecting an announcement directly from the senator shortly," said the newswoman. "In fact, let's take you live to the press conference now."

The car filled with the sound of microphone feedback and clicking cameras. And then a hush fell over the crowd of reporters as the senator began to speak.

"Good evening," he said with his usually steady voice. "I stand before you today in a time of uncertainty, not only for our campaign, but for the trust and faith you have placed in me. A moment that calls for clarity and truth. It has been brought to my attention that a member of our campaign team has been arrested on serious charges. I want to be clear, right here and now, that I am as shocked and disturbed as you are by this revelation.

"I entered public service driven by a profound sense of duty to serve the people, to uphold the laws of our great nation, and to relentlessly pursue the betterment of our communities. The trust you have placed in me is something I value above all else, and I want to assure you, I have not —and I will not —let this trust be compromised.

"The individual arrested was a member of a large and dedicated team, each with specific tasks and responsibilities. I am not involved in every aspect of their work and, as such, had no knowledge of any illegal activities that may have been conducted. I am deeply saddened by this incident, but I am even more determined to ensure that this does not happen again.

"In response to this occurrence, I have ordered an immediate internal review of our campaign practices and procedures. This includes a thorough investigation to establish the facts and ensure transparency. In this process, we will cooperate fully with law enforcement officials, sharing any information that might help their investigations. We stand by the principles of justice, and if there has been wrongdoing, those responsible must face the consequences of their actions.

"However, I stand here today not just to address this unfortunate event, but to reaffirm my unwavering commitment to serving you. Our campaign has been, and will always be, about the people, about your needs, your hopes, and your dreams. It is about championing the causes that matter to you and driving policies that uplift our communities.

"This incident does not define us. Our strength lies in our ability to stand together, face challenges, and overcome them. The actions of one individual do not reflect the dedication, passion, and commitment of the thousands of team members who work tirelessly every day for a better future.

"We are in the midst of an important campaign, a campaign that matters to us all. It is an opportunity to set the course for our future, to shape our society in ways that reflect our values and ambitions. I promise you, this incident will not deter us from our goal. It will not divert our focus. We will continue to fight for what we believe in.

"In closing, I want to assure you that I am more committed than ever to this campaign and to the service of the public. I will not let this incident overshadow our mission or compromise our goals. We have important work ahead of us, and together, we will rise above this challenge. I am forever grateful for your support, for your trust, and for your belief in our shared vision. Let us move forward together, with renewed dedication and unfaltering resolve."

Tracy reached for the radio and turned down the volume.

"Jesus," she said. "Can you believe this guy?"

Jimmy scratched his jaw.

"Yeah, well, what can you do? Some people smell shit and think it's honeysuckle."

She looked at him.

"Do you really think he had nothing to do with Dana Brockers' murder? Or Tony's?"

He shrugged.

"Honestly? I really don't know. He may have ordered both killings. Or he may really just be a pawn in some greater game. If you want my advice, it's best not to think about it. That applies to most things in life, to be honest."

She shook her head.

"It doesn't feel like justice."

He raised his eyebrows.

"You caught the killer," he said. "And you're not dead. Although it's certainly not for a lack of trying. Anyway, in this world, that's what I call justice. And this is the only world there is. Now, do you have my money?"

She shook her head and handed him an envelope. She watched as he took it and considered its weight.

"I put some extra in there," she said. "Consider it a retainer."

He raised his eyebrows.

"I work alone."

She smiled slightly.

"Yeah. Me too."

They sat a while longer, their eyes drifting back to the radio, which murmured with a furious commotion of low indecipherable voices.

"Can you really do any good in this world?" she asked. "I mean, how do you stand against people with that much power? They win every time."

He looked at her.

"Nah," he said. "They only win if you stop trying. And you don't strike me as the type to quit. Even when you should."

She looked at him, and he almost seemed to blush as he cracked open the door and put a foot outside the car.

"Are you still trying?" she asked.

"Nope," he said.

She watched as he got out of the car.

"But keep my number anyway," he said. "I could always use a few extra bucks."

She smiled as he shut the door and walked away into the night.

When he was gone, she looked down at the radio and listened to the ranting voices trying to make sense of the world.

But after a while, it just seemed like noise. So, she turned up the radio and spun the dial until it settled on something that made sense. And the music filled the car and warmed her soul while she sat back in her seat and made a slow and peaceful drive home.

The End

Also by RJ Law and available at Amazon:
DROWNED AT DAWN (Tracy Sterling Book 3)

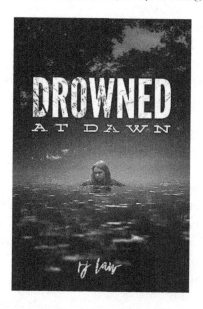

Hey there! Join my VIP Reader's Club.
You'll get exclusive promotions, complimentary goodies and other special surprises.
Visit www.rjlawbooks.com to join for free — I hope to see you there!

A Request from the Author:

Dear friend,

I rely on reviews to get the word out about my books. If you enjoyed this story, can I ask you to take a moment to leave a brief review on Amazon?

You can leave a quick customer review at the bottom of the page at https://www.amazon.com/dp/B0CB4XR2P3/

Thank you so much for reading. I hope you enjoyed this book as much as I enjoyed writing it. Readers like you are what keeps me writing and I thank you for your support.

All the best to you and yours.

RJ LAW

Made in United States
North Haven, CT
16 March 2024

50085062R00098